"Go Back To The Party, Princess."

His throat was taut, his voice guttural. "Do the things debutantes do. You don't want me. I'm too old for you."

"Poor ancient Ben. What is it? Nine years? Are you nine whole years older than I?"

"Princess." He didn't look at her; he didn't dare. "You've mistaken friendship for something more."

"I'm not that young, or that foolish. I haven't confused caring for love. But you could make believe. Would it be so hard, Ben?" She hesitated. "Just for one evening, couldn't you pretend you love me?"

Pretend! He'd spent two years loving her, watching, fascinated, as she bloomed into womanhood. Now she stood before him asking for make-believe! He drew a shuddering breath. "For your own sake, Victoria, you should leave. Now."

"It was for my sake that I came."

Dear Reader,

Welcome to Silhouette! Our goal is to give you hours of unbeatable reading pleasure, and we hope you'll enjoy each month's six new Silhouette Desires. These sensual, provocative love stories are both believable and compelling—sometimes they're poignant, sometimes humorous, but always enjoyable.

Indulge yourself. Experience all the passion and excitement of falling in love along with our heroine as she meets the irresistible man of her dreams and together they overcome all obstacles in the path to a happy ending.

If this is your first Desire, I hope it'll be the first of many. If you're already a Silhouette Desire reader, thanks for your support! Look for some of your favorite authors in the coming months: Stephanie James, Diana Palmer, Dixie Browning, Ann Major and Doreen Owens Malek, to name just a few.

Happy reading!

Isabel Swift
Senior Editor

SDRL-7/85

BJ JAMES
The Sound of Goodbye

Silhouette Desire

Published by Silhouette Books New York

America's Publisher of Contemporary Romance

SILHOUETTE BOOKS
300 East 42nd St., New York, N.Y. 10017

Copyright © 1987 by BJ James

ISBN: 0-373-05332-0

First Silhouette Books printing February 1987

America's Publisher of Contemporary Romance

Printed in the U.S.A.

BJ JAMES

married her high school sweetheart straight out of college and soon found that books were delightful companions during her lonely nights as a doctor's wife. Her life is filled with her loving husband and family, pets, writing...and romance.

To the ladies from Georgia, Maryland and Texas,
with my thanks.

One

There was no light but moonlight. It spilled palely through bare French doors and only the hum of an ornate ceiling fan rippled the stillness. Then, in the gloom, a cigarette glowed.

On a rumpled bed a young man lay, one arm bent comfortably beneath his head. He drew the cigarette back to his lips, inhaled deeply, exhaled, and watched the smoke slowly dissipate. A distant shout of youthful laughter rose, faltered, ebbed. In the silence his hand dropped lazily to his bare midriff.

His heavy eyelids drifted down, sweeping lean cheeks with dark lashes. A second trill of muffled laughter went unnoticed, and the forgotten cigarette consumed itself. The steady rise and fall of his even breathing, the slack lines of his body, his carelessness, suggested "one last glass" of champagne had, indeed, been too much.

A door opened, then shut cautiously, its sharp click rousing him. He glanced groggily with unfocused eyes at his watch.

"Damn!" The expletive rumbled suddenly and hoarsely in his throat as the heat from a glowing ash brought him completely awake. In a smooth rolling motion he sat on the side of the bed, stabbing out the last of the fire in a crystal ashtray on the nightstand.

"You really shouldn't smoke in bed, Ben." A lilting laugh accompanied the teasing words.

Startled, he turned, aware for the first time that he was not alone. A girl dressed in white stood before the door. Ben's frown deepened, scoring a face turned ashen with taut, brooding lines. From thin, unsmiling lips his harsh demand slashed at her. "Victoria! What in hell are you doing here?"

With a toss of her head she flipped her loose hair from her shoulders, then leaned back against the beveled glass of the square panes. Her eyes traveled over him from bare feet to rumpled slacks, lingering at the dark hair that curled over his chest. When her gaze collided with his, she chuckled. "I've come to see you, of course. Why else would I be in your room?"

"A room in your parents' guesthouse," he corrected. "You know you shouldn't be here. They wouldn't approve."

"Ahh. Wouldn't they, now?" She shrugged. The deeply cut neckline of her gown dipped provocatively lower over the curve of her breasts and the shadowed cleft between. A chain glinted gold as a delicate heart swayed from it, touching her, caressing her, as it nestled in that secret place.

"What do you want?" His voice was edged with strain as he fought a familiar battle. She was lovely. Her smooth skin glowed warm and dusky. As it captured the beam of a full moon, her brown hair shimmered with a burnished gold of its own. The fabric of her designer gown clung to the lush contours of her body.

He wanted her. He ached for her. He had for a long time...but he knew she was not for him.

In the separate worlds of Victoria Mallory, daughter of a powerful man, and Ben Stockton, employee, there could be no common ground. None. He'd attended this last festivity of the so-called season by invitation, a summons not to be denied. He'd obeyed as he must; Ben, attractive, brilliant, innovative, eligible, yet not suitable.

Throughout the long weekend he'd watched her, devouring her, drinking and smoking his way through social amenities that bored him. No matter how he resisted, he'd been constantly drawn to her, until the hurtful void of what could not be had driven him to the solitude of his room.

Now she'd come, and in the dimness he could sense a strangeness. The cool reserve she wore like a cloak had vanished. As she leaned indolently against the rich wood, the murky air about her seemed to smolder with an untamed recklessness, something wild and undefinable. She was danger, and tonight he hadn't the strength to resist her.

Ben wet his lips with the tip of his tongue, cursing the cottony dryness left by too many cigarettes and too much drink. In a cold voice betraying none of his torment, his question became a demand. "I asked you what you want."

"Ben, you surprise me." The sound of her hushed laughter was a sensuous music. "Surely you know...." Her gown swayed alluringly about her at each drawn breath, and he heard again that rough velvet purring deep in her throat. "I want the same thing the other girls want when they visit your room. I want you."

"Don't be ridiculous!" He was stunned by her directness. Steeling himself, with exaggerated care he shook another cigarette from the pack. The flare of his lighter illuminated the carved planes of his face, emphasizing the sharp jut of his square jaw. He inhaled long and hard then sat studying the fiery tip.

Slowly he raised his head. With intended insolence his eyes roved over her. Quirking his lips into a cruel smile, he stared with suggestive thoroughness at the décolleté that displayed the slope of her breasts. Like a marauder stripping the clothing from her, he explored every line of her body. When his gaze at last returned to meet hers, harsh laughter twisted his dark features into a sneer. "You're just a baby. You haven't the slightest idea what you're saying."

"Haven't I?" Patient amusement was in her smile. "I know what you're doing, but it won't work. You're not the sort of man you've just pretended, and we both know it. You've been my friend." Her laughter rippled. "You're no lecher, Ben."

"Go away, princess. Friend or not, I don't play with children." He stretched out on the bed, staring up at the monotonous motion of the fan in feigned indifference.

"Ahh, there you have it. The crux of the matter. I'm eighteen, hardly a child. And if I must be the princess, then for just this once I claim her rights."

Her gown rustled as she stepped away from the door. In spite of himself he looked at her as she stood bathed in the silvery light. She was all he'd dreamed of and wanted for the past two years.

"No," he muttered, wiping the beads of perspiration from his forehead. He knew he should get up, that he should take her bodily to the door, but a wave of vertigo washed over him and he knew he couldn't.

"Yes," she said. "Tomorrow my engagement will be announced. In two months I'll be married to a man of my father's choosing. A fit consort for the princess." An edge of bitterness crept into her voice. She sighed, then, in resignation. "Tomorrow Caroline will begin her campaign for you, and what Caroline wants, Caroline gets."

Victoria took one step toward the bed. "But that's tomorrow. Until then there are no ties that bind us." One more step brought her closer still. In a whisper barely heard she said, "Whatever we share tonight can't hurt anyone."

"Go back to the party, princess." His throat was taut, his voice guttural. "Do the things debutantes do. You don't want me. I'm too old for you."

"Poor ancient Ben. What is it? Nine years? Are you nine whole years older than I?"

"Princess." He didn't look at her; he dared not. "You've mistaken friendship for something more."

"I'm not that young, nor that foolish. I haven't confused caring for love. But we could make believe. Would it be so hard, Ben?" She hesitated. "Just for one magical evening, couldn't you pretend that you love me?"

Pretend! He'd spent two years feeling the fool, loving her, watching, fascinated, as she bloomed into womanhood. Now she stood before him asking for make-believe!

Ben drew a shuddering breath, his face a somber mask. "For your own sake, Victoria, you should leave. Now."

"It was for my sake that I came."

"You don't understand what you're doing."

"Don't I?"

"You've had too much champagne."

"Not as much as you, my friend," she teased.

"Dammit!" He cursed again his intemperance. "I know I've had too much to drink. That's even more reason for you to leave. I'm not thinking clearly. Princess—"

"My proper Ben. Always in control. Always so sure of himself." Then, in intuitive acknowledgement of the edge of desperation in his voice, she murmured, "Until now."

The hand she'd been holding behind her back lifted to the zipper beneath her shoulders. Its sliding rasp was thunderous in the quiet. Her gown parted and fell away. Inch by agonizing inch the delicate shield of satin and lace slipped to her waist, unveiling her unbound breasts. Every nerve in Ben's body tensed. He'd known she would be beautiful, but he hadn't expected such perfection. This vision before him was more than he had ever thought to have. He wanted to hold her, touch her, caress her.

As he watched helplessly, paralyzed by the power of his desire, a slight undulation of her slender hips sent the lacy sheath slithering from her body. She stepped carelessly out of it, her breasts swaying as she kicked free of her shoes. Clad only in panties and golden chain, she stood before him. Waiting.

"No, princess," Ben groaned. "Please."

"Please what, Ben? What're you really asking?" Her voice flowed over him, drawing him deeper into the madness.

He couldn't move. He lay caught in the web she'd spun. The space that separated them throbbed with a new fierceness. Still she waited. A flicker of uncertainty passed over her face, bringing her brows down into a faint frown. Her eyes closed briefly: a tiny shiver seized her. Then, as though she had settled something in her mind for the last time, her expression cleared. She brushed back the heavy fall of her hair and moved with a proud, measured step to his bedside.

Victoria stood gazing down at him, savoring the sound of the ragged breath he could not calm. The look of him offered hope for a moment of fulfillment, a small triumph over the loneliness of her future. With her head bent toward him there was a regal splendor about her and no shred of uncertainty. "For just this once, Ben, I want to be the princess with all the rights it entails. I claim *droit du seigneur*. I claim a night of love with the man of my choosing. As a scholar you should understand the custom."

"You have the wrong century, the wrong country, the wrong sex, and this isn't a wedding night." He could hardly think. To speak had been an effort.

Beyond the light she was a moving shadow as darkness sculpted in mystery the curves and hollows of her body. She'd become an illusion, a mystical enchantress who drew him to the brink of obsession. Yet he knew that if he touched her she would be warm and exciting and very real.

Ben knew that he should leave the bed, that he should turn away from her, but he knew he wouldn't. He couldn't.

"What're you thinking?" she asked. "Of peasants and nobles and their whims? Are you thinking that ancient traditions have no place in the present?" Her teasing mood disappeared. "For once you'd be wrong. Does the country matter so long as all else is right? Shall we call it *droit du seigneura*? Invent a new name for an old custom and consider it the privilege of the liberated?

"Names don't matter, Ben. Only this night matters. It's the right time. The only time. For me it will be the wedding night." The bed dipped beneath her as she sat by his side. "You'll burn yourself," she murmured, taking the long-ashed stub from his fingers. As she leaned to discard it, her fragrance surrounded him in an intoxicating aura.

Cool fingers stroked his fevered skin. Her hand was steady, her face calm, but her eyes were not. Their golden brown depths were pleading and afraid, and strangely hurt.

"Please," she whispered as she touched the side of his face. "Do this for me. Let me learn about love from one who sees me as more than a pawn in a merger. Be tender and make the loving wonderful. I can stand whatever follows, as long as the first time is beautiful. Teach me, Ben." There was the hint of tears in her voice, a lost look in her eyes, and Ben would have given his world to wipe away the sadness.

"Princess," he sighed, and in defeat he touched her. His hands at her shoulders drew her down to him. Her sharp shivering gasp blended with his low groan as her bare skin met his in a world of new sensations. For a long while he only embraced her, waiting for the trembling to subside.

When she quieted, relaxing against him, his fingers began to drift over her. Stroking, soothing, he murmured disjointed phrases of assurance. He raised his arms and turned her pliant body, her hair swirling about her. In the space of a sigh she lay against the pillow, wide-eyed and still.

Ben allowed himself one kiss, a taste of promised sweetness, then stood to discard the last of his clothing. When he returned to the bed he saw she hadn't moved. Her eyes were on him, wandering, touching his nakedness, in anticipation. Looking into their golden flecks, he wondered which might hurt her more, rejection or what was to come.

Bending over her, he stroked her lips with his fingers. "Are you sure you want this?"

She nodded, never looking away from him.

"You're frightened." His heart contracted at the realization. "It took every bit of courage you could muster to come to me, didn't it?"

She swallowed convulsively and nodded again.

"I hadn't realized until tonight what an accomplished actress you were," he teased her lightly, hoping to bring a smile to her rigid lips.

"I've been acting all my life, Ben. Until tonight." Victoria said quietly.

"And if I hadn't been so willingly charmed, what would you have done?" he asked hoarsely.

"I don't know." Then, meeting his look, she whispered, "I think perhaps anything."

"Oh, God!" Passions flared; she'd destroyed the last of his restraint. "The love of a man for a woman can be beautiful. It will be, princess. I promise."

Trembling with barely contained hunger, he began a slow, sweet seduction. With consummate skill he caressed her, touching her brow, stroking a velvet eyelid, brushing against the long lashes as they rested on her cheeks. The satin of her skin enchanted him. Like a blind man whose memories lay in his fingertips, he learned her face.

He leaned to touch her cheek with his own, careful not to mark her with the abrasive stubble of his beard. Though she'd been submissive to his touch, when his trail of kisses led to her lips he found them cold and stiff. He understood. The last of her courage in tatters, she brought to him the inhibitions of a sheltered life. For all her willingness, they wouldn't be easily cast aside.

Ben made no demands. He played the teasing lover until her lips softened, accepting the slanting pressure of his own. Until her eyes clung to his. Until her breath became a sigh as she rose to meet kiss with kiss.

He reveled in her new abandon, and with each halting response he retreated, only to return again and again, finding each new surrender more delightful than the last. Tenderly he led her with him deeper into an inferno, sure in the knowledge that he could die of thirst for her. An ague of need convulsed him. Burying his face in hair of spun silk, inhaling its clean fragrance, he fought to curb the desire that had been his companion for two long years.

Go slowly, he cautioned himself with the vestiges of a waning strength. Far more than the appeasing of his own desperate needs, he wanted to take her gently into the ecstasy that loving could be. But the body does not always listen to the heart, and he grew taut in the battle he fought.

For Victoria there was pleasure in the weight of him and in the pounding of his heart against her breast. He was as she'd known he would be, the virile male, beautiful and excitingly aroused. His breath against her hair was the sweetest delight, the touch of his heated flesh a treasure.

He was beautiful and had given her much, but she would have more. The wonder of Ben, her joy of him, had banished the fearful girl. In her stead was one who stood poised at the brink, no longer child, not yet woman, hungering with a burning impatience for what was so nearly within her reach.

She sensed his hesitancy, and with an inborn wisdom she responded. Her seeking fingers stealing into his hair, threading through the shining blackness of the crisp strands, drew him closer in silent invitation. His answering sigh stirred a tremor deep inside her; a rapturous warmth flooded over her as he lifted his mouth to hers. His seeking kiss devoured her. When his tongue entreated, her lips parted eagerly. Yielding to his conquest, she gave herself into his keeping.

"Princess," he said. Untangling from her hair, his hands glided to her breast. At his first discovering caress she breathed a quiet sound of pleasure and contentment. Cupping her fullness in his palm, he bent to her. As the nipple contracted beneath the first feathery pull of his tongue, she tensed. He moved away, and with aching patience he waited. For a breathless moment she seemed to withdraw and he dared not move, then her fingers tightened in his hair, drawing him back to her arching breasts. With a broken cry he took the tiny bud into his mouth, and his desperately controlled desire broke forever from its bounds.

In a touch that was exquisitely light, his hands skimmed over her, coming to rest at her hip. He knelt at her side and with infinite care removed the final barrier. She was golden brown and sun kissed, beautiful beyond description.

Boldly, his hand traced a path of fire over the flat planes of her belly, lingered, brushed lightly over the tightly coiled curls below, then moved slowly to the firm line of her thigh. A half smile curved her lips as she accepted the gentleness of his touch. He kissed the knee that bore a half-moon scar left by some childish transgression, and she found his lips against her flesh as welcome as before.

Victoria, petitioner in the guise of seductress, became instead an apt pupil. She met each intimate caress in kind. Her eloquent hands ignited in him a maddening excitement. Her body sang for him a siren's song, one he could no more resist than he could cease to breathe.

Holding her, searching out her wondrous mysteries, he discovered a world that was new. He'd never loved any woman. There had never been for him such desire. Victoria's touch was like none he'd ever known, and this night would live forever in his memory. It was the first and only time she would be his.

Deliciously unhurried, his hand slid over her sleek skin in the last and most intimate caress. The prelude had come to an end.

"Ben?" It was only his name, spoken in her vibrant voice, but it was the final plea.

"Yes, love, now." He rose over her, aching, denying his own savage needs. He would be gentle, teaching her what love could be. What he could give her.

In a last coherent thought, as teacher became lover, he wondered at his madness. Was this intoxication? An innate honesty allowed only the truth: he'd been sober from the first moment she'd touched him. Truth. Damnation or acquittal? He no longer knew as he led her reverently into womanhood.

As she moved to welcome him, there was no outcry. There was only Ben and Victoria joining together in an unpretended love. But for a suspended moment time flew, becoming thief, destroyer, enemy. It had no place in their loving, yet its passing brought with it contentment.

Victoria's long hair swirled over him, wrapping him in a tawny cascade, shimmering in golden contrast to the dark thatch that shaded his chest. Her cheek rested against him. Only her fingers moved restlessly, burrowing into the wiry curls as if to memorize his body.

As Ben bent to kiss the top of her head, the cool slide of a tear mingled with the beads of moisture that marked his heated body in a silver sheen. His hand under her chin, he lifted her face to his searching gaze. "Regrets, princess?"

"No regrets." She smiled through her tears. Her face hid nothing; its soft, warm glow held his answer.

"Are you sure?" he asked, eager to hear her speak what he read in her shining eyes. "You won't be sorry?"

"Never! You've given me a time to cherish. No matter what happens now, tonight can't be taken from me."

"Then why this?" He brushed away a glistening drop.

"Because I'm one of those silly people who cries when she's happy." She added softly, "I've never been so happy."

"Nor have I." His hands moved over her body possessively, drawing her close. He wanted to keep her with him, to deny tomorrow.

"Was it wrong of me to steal this night?"

"Nothing so beautiful could be wrong."

"It's nearly dawn," she murmured, comforted. "Hold me, Ben, just for a little longer. Until morning comes."

His hand wove through her hair and drew her head to his chest. Her body curled into his with a natural ease. He held her, staring at a black sky that awaited the crimson of dawn. Stillness crept over the room, and for a time only the sounds of their breathing could be heard.

From the dense foliage of a nearby forest a night-bird sang a soft farewell. Victoria stirred. The swell of her breast brushed against Ben and he woke.

The blurred radiance of early morning crept into every shadowed corner of the room, bringing with it anger. He'd meant to hold her through the night, treasuring each precious moment, but the sweet fatigue of fulfillment had defeated him. With hot, burning eyes he watched the relentless birth of a new day and grieved for what he'd lost.

Victoria stirred again, and instinctively his fingers closed on her shoulder. She tensed but said nothing. Then, as he recognized the uselessness of it, he relaxed his grip, and his hand slid away to lie limply against the sheet.

In a rapid move, Victoria rose. Ben watched as she gathered her scattered clothing and began to dress. The slither of fabric and the growl of the zipper recalled a vivid memory, and with it the ache of despair. He closed his eyes as he listened to the sounds of goodbye.

He knew when she came to stand over him. He felt the brush of her hand over his hair and the touch of her lips against his forehead. He knew when she moved away. He heard her light tread as she crossed the room. It was the unmistakable sound of an opening door that destroyed his resolve to let her go.

"Can you do this, Victoria? Can you go to him after last night?" The question ripped from him. His eyes were on her. He saw her stiffen, saw her fingers tighten around the brass knob of the door. "Can you be his wife now?"

She leaned her head against the flat edge of the door. The silence while he waited was agony. When she raised her head to meet his gaze, her eyes were lifeless. Yet even as he watched she changed. A subtle transformation, the power of an inner strength, wiped the distress from her face. Acceptance of the inevitable brought with it peace.

"Yes." Ben didn't want to hear, but her empty voice droned on. "I can marry Carlos. Even now."

"But . . ." He stopped, quieted by the slow shake of her head.

"Carlos wants this merger, and I'm a part of it. He won't care that we've been lovers. He's already warned me he has no intention of giving up his mistresses. He has no time for frightened young virgins." She laughed mirthlessly. "Perhaps he'll even thank you for what you've taught me."

"Victoria—"

"Goodbye, Ben," she whispered, cutting short his protest. "I'll never forget you."

"Victoria!" His answer was the metallic click of the closing door. For a long while he stared, numb and unbelieving, at the gleaming panes. He had taken her in love and given himself in return, and she'd walked away.

His eyes were drawn to the rumpled covers that surrounded him and to a long thread of glinting gold that lay tangled in a pool of crimson. In exchange for the heart and the love he'd offered, she'd left a heart of gold and her virgin blood. It was then that he truly believed she was gone.

As his hand closed over the broken necklace, the unicorn captured within the misshapen circlet mocked him, a reminder that soon she would lie in the arms of another man.

* * *

It was late. Only Ben remained in the deserted office. With tie loose, shirt sleeves rolled back and hair disheveled by fingers that raked it constantly, he sat before his orderly desk. On its polished surface lay a pen, a sheet of paper, one word scrawled across it: *Victoria*.

It had been the same for the past three weeks. Ben spent long hours at his work, seeking to wipe her from his mind through exhaustion. And each day was like the last. He waited, hoping she would come to him. Every laugh he heard became her low chuckle, every drift of perfume recalled hers, every blank page invited her name.

"Fool!" He crumpled the paper. "She isn't coming to you. She never intended to. She wanted from you exactly what she took, one night, no more." Even as he cursed himself, his gaze was turning to the chair that faced him. How many times had she sat there? How many hours had they talked and laughed while she waited for her father? Who knew her hopes and dreams better than he?

From the day he'd first seen her, she'd filled his thoughts, and from that day he'd known it was hopeless. She'd been sixteen, the only child of wealthy parents. Her father was king of commerce, her home the castle and she its princess. He was twenty-five and, for all his brilliance, from the wrong side of town. Perfect for the company, but not for the princess. Yet against these odds their friendship flourished. It was with Ben she shared her dreams. It was Victoria he told of his ambitions. And never once as she listened raptly, had he forgotten how lovely she was, or that they could never be more than friends.

"Once," he muttered as he tossed the paper into the trash. "I forgot once!" His hand closed in a crushing grip over the pen, impotent in despair over a moment of weakness that could never be recalled. The worry that gnawed constantly at the back of his mind surfaced. His lips curled in renewed disgust when he remembered how careless he'd been. What if . . .

"No!" He turned his chair to look bleakly out at the summer evening. It couldn't happen. Not in this day of the informed, the age of sophisticated medicine. Victoria was to be married soon, and for all her innocence she was not naive.

"But what if . . ." The pen broke, spilling ink over his fingers.

"Stockton?" Ben turned to face Clayton Mallory, who stood, impatient and arrogant, in the doorway. "I stopped by my office and found this memo that you asked to see me tomorrow. Since we're both here, why don't we handle whatever your little problem is now?"

The words were coolly imperious and, by habit, condescending. Ben's remorse, his self-recriminations, his torment, coalesced into a bitter hatred. Unreasoning as it was unrelenting, it became a scabrous protection for the wounds of guilt as well as rejection. A distaste for all things Mallory rose like bile in Ben's throat and an indecision was resolved. His face was bland as he nodded in agreement. "I suppose now is as good a time as any. Since my little problem isn't a problem any longer, it shouldn't take long."

"Good." Clayton Mallory glanced at his watch. "We do have dinner guests coming at eight."

This man uses me, Ben thought as he observed the elegantly dressed Clayton cross to the comfortable chair before the desk. My mind is bought and paid for, and as long as I have anything to offer he'll suck it dry.

But once I stop being useful he'll toss me aside without a qualm.

"Like father, like daughter," Ben snarled in a low voice, and in that hour he believed it.

"I beg your pardon?"

"Just thinking aloud," Ben said negligently. He carefully drew a handkerchief from his pocket and wiped the ink from his hand. When he finished and the handkerchief had served its purpose, he discarded it. As Victoria had discarded Ben himself once he'd served his purpose. An unwelcome image of frightened tawny eyes and a soft pleading voice battered at the fortress of his newborn malice, but he pushed it away.

"Really, my dear boy, I haven't the time to sit and listen to you think aloud," Mallory drawled in a wry humor, setting Ben's teeth on edge.

"Then I won't waste any more of your time. I'm resigning."

"You're what?" The graceful carelessness of the older man's attitude evaporated.

"I'm resigning," Ben repeated. "If you insist, I'll work a notice, but I'd like it to be effective immediately."

"You can't resign!"

"I can and I am."

"We'll need you in the merger."

"Anyone can do that as well as I, or nearly as well," Ben said honestly.

"You have another offer, I suppose," Mallory said coldly and unnecessarily, for it was common knowledge that Ben had had many offers.

"For some time a friend has asked my help in a new venture. I've decided to accept the challenge."

Clayton Mallory folded his hands beneath his chin, one finger tapping thoughtfully against his grim lips. He looked hard into Ben's unflinching eyes. "What about Victoria? She's not exactly overjoyed at some of the ramifications of this merger. She seems to relate well to you. I had hoped you would . . . ah . . . help her through this."

Ben realized then that the perceptive man knew how he felt about Victoria and wouldn't hesitate to turn it to his advantage. How I felt, *past tense*, Ben amended. "Victoria doesn't need me. Not anymore."

"Perhaps she doesn't need you." Mallory paused, then glided smoothly on, taking another tack. "But you're the best friend she has. If you leave, she'll miss you."

"She'll get over it," Ben said shortly. There was an implacable coldness in him that forestalled argument.

Clayton Mallory had not become the successful man he was by wasting time on lost causes. With practiced grace he accepted the inevitable. "So be it." He rose and walked to the open door, then paused. "When will you be leaving?"

Ben spun his chair around and looked out over the familiar, sprawling landscape of Riverton for the last time. He knew he would miss it. "I'll clear out my desk before I leave tonight."

"Fine. Will you be saying goodbye to Victoria?"

"No."

The word was swallowed by a deepening silence, and after a minute Ben realized he was alone. Like an old man whose joints ached and creaked with the effort, he turned and began to methodically gather his personal belongings. In a surprisingly short time he had finished. There was little he would be taking with him. Requiring absolutely no space in his briefcase was the most important thing: a lesson well learned. No woman would ever hurt him again. His heart would be his own. If there was any using, it would be mutual.

At twenty-seven, Ben was still young enough to believe his righteous anger was directed solely at Victoria. As his eyes swept the office one last time, he could still deny the hard core of guilt resting deeply in his subconscious, a guilt that would be added fuel for an unreasonable hate.

When he closed the door behind him in the deepening darkness, he believed he had put this all behind him, that the Mallorys could never touch him again.

Months later, when the tabloids feasted at the expense of the Mallorys, Ben was still telling himself it meant nothing to him. Of what consequence was it to him that the merger was accomplished but the marriage postponed, or that after months of traveling abroad Victoria had suddenly disappeared without a trace? Even as he devoured detailed reports based strictly on supposition, he convinced himself he did not care. When capricious fate dealt the final blow, he discovered he was not as hardened as he thought. He mourned Clayton and Elizabeth Mallory as the sensational news of their deaths in the fiery crash of their private plane eclipsed the abandoned search for their daughter. In time he sickened on the carnival of conjecture as the uninformed ran amok. None was more thankful than he when their tragedy was laid to rest, eclipsed again by a newer, fresher sensation.

"It's over," Ben said with a finality as he folded the month-old newspaper he'd read into tatters. Lost in his memories, he slumped in his chair as the neon sign of the motel flashed hypnotically through the window. He had no idea how long he'd sat remembering, dredging up the hurts that were suddenly unimportant, when a tentative tap shook the ill-fitting door on its hinges.

"Who on earth?" He expected no one: in his travels for his fledgling company he'd had little time for friends. The sight at his doorstep stopped him short. A small man, dressed in such painful care that it bordered on prim, stood with his hand raised to tap once more.

"What can I do for you?" Ben's tone was gruffer than he'd intended.

"Benjamin Stockton?" Looking past Ben into the shabby room, the little man said doubtfully, "Benjamin Alfred Stockton?"

"Guilty." Ben was amused at the nervous birdlike manner of his caller.

"Phinias T. Crowe—" he tugged at an already perfectly adjusted tie "—investigator with social services. Your partner said I would find you here."

Ben failed to stifle a smile at the name as he gestured toward the object of Crowe's disdain. "All the comforts of home, at least for another week. Won't you come in?"

"That will hardly be necessary. I have here a document we would like you to sign." As if by magic, he produced the paper.

The grin playing over his lips, Ben took it from him. As he read, his smile froze, then faded. "What the hell? Is this a mistake, or is it somebody's idea of a joke?"

"It's no mistake, and no joke, I assure you." Phinias fished a pen from his briefcase. "If you would just sign on the lines indicated, I'll be on my way."

"Sign?" Ben's voice was a low grating whisper, his lips a grim line in his drawn face. "Sign! If you think for one minute I'm going to sign this paper, Mr. Phinias T. Crowe, then you're as crazy as I feel right now."

"Then—" the perfect tie was adjusted once more "—I suppose I must accept your...ah...hospitality so the matter can be discussed. Rationally."

Precisely forty-five minutes later, a ruffled Phinias T. Crowe took his leave, following a discussion that was somewhat less than rational. In the dark of his room Ben watched the flashing sign blindly, his mind miles away and in the past. He had been wrong once more; it was not over. The Mallorys had touched him again, this time binding him irrevocably to them.

Later, he tossed his battered suitcase onto the rumpled bed and began to pack. For the first time in months he was going home.

Two

———

High above the horizon the castle soared, casting its image like a shadow over the deep water of the lake. No current stirred; no ripple distorted. Like a jewel it gleamed, its towering granite and massive timbers repeated in glittering reflection. Then, in a milli-second of soft sound, stone and wood exploded, bursting into droplets that flashed in sunlight like a scattering of rubies. Water churned, calmed, then in its stillness the castle endured.

One by one a gathering of small pebbles clattered harmlessly on the grassy shore, and a slender young woman turned to face a castle of substance. It was as she remembered. Not a stone or a tree or a blade of grass seemed altered in the long years of her absence. It survived as those who inhabited it had not.

All it lacked was a princess.

There had been a princess once. Memories of that sad young girl rose, haunting, hurting, and a bitter smile quirked her grim lips. There had been a princess. One who'd had everything yet nothing. One worshipped but unloved. One pampered, neglected, suffocated, destroyed. A possession to barter in the lustful search for power.

Bleak eyes roved over walls that had surrounded her in a prison of beauty. Beautiful still, but her prison no more. With a dismissive gesture she shifted, her gaze at last falling on the cottage gracing the well-kept grounds like a small and perfect haven. The harshness of her expression softened; the ache in her heart eased. Here there had been a moment of love and of happiness. Happiness and loving as complete and as fleeting as it had been creative.

Another memory stirred, a new pain surfaced, one never forgotten, never subdued. She waited with fists clenched by her side and head bowed before the onslaught. It came as it always came, and as always she was left ravaged and trembling. Then in its wake, from the depths of courage, she found the strength to put memories behind her. She did not look again at the cottage; she dared not.

Slowly she returned to the present and to the lake, to face her own image, reproduced relentlessly by shimmering water. Her lips moved in an imitation of a smile. Even as it glistened in the light, her reflection was lackluster. She had forgotten how thin she'd become. Nor had she cared that her hair was dull and drab or that hollows fell like shadows beneath her cheekbones. Yet in the eyes that gazed back at her, deep-set with the bruised look of fatigue, there was hard-won serenity that the ache of ancient loss could not quell.

She looked down at herself, at the scrupulously clean but tattered jeans, at the frayed linen shirt that had once carried a designer label, and finally at her sandals, handmade, plainly sturdy, and scuffed from her dusty walk. Uncommon dress for royalty, she thought with a joyless chuckle.

The image of a young girl dressed in white lace with a golden heart glittering at her breast filled her mind. Despite her efforts of before, there was a sudden shine of tears on her lashes. She closed her eyelids to guard against the spill as a mindless jingle echoed in her head.

Long live the princess. Where is the princess? The princess has come home.

"The princess has come home."

At the harsh sound of a voice from her past she whirled. "Ben?"

"Victoria." He acknowledged her with a curt nod. No emotion registered in his bland face as he stood on the slope of the lakeshore.

"I didn't hear you come up."

"My car's down by the road. I was on my way home when I saw you standing here. I walked across the field."

"Home?" Victoria frowned. There were no houses here. Only the castle and its surrounding buildings.

She hadn't the time to realize no answer was given to her half-formed question as belated shock rocketed through her, robbing her of all sense of reason. Was he real, or was this chance encounter a cruel trick of imagination? She closed her eyes, then slowly, almost dreadfully, she opened them. The sting of strain eased; her vision sharpened. Her mind accepted. He was flesh; he was blood. He was Ben.

At first she thought he hadn't changed, this man who had once been the center of the girlish fantasies of Victoria Mallory. Now she could see that time had left its mark with kindness. How old was he? It had been eight years; he would be thirty-five.

In those years he'd added muscle, filling out broad shoulders and a wide chest that had once been more bone than flesh, leaving waist and thighs as trim as before. A bit under six feet, with his brawny leanness he exuded power that could diminish larger men. The touch of early gray at his temples was an added distinction to the maturity he wore with assurance. Ben Stockton had become the man he'd been destined to be.

Even dressed casually, tie gone and shirt sleeves folded back, he was rigid and distant. But he hadn't always been. Victoria remembered that he'd been filled with the fire of passion once, and she'd been real for the first time in her life. Never forgotten, the moment had been her talisman, her strength to survive the years that followed.

She wanted to go to him, to tousle his thick black hair and draw his lips to hers, supplanting a memory with reality. The need was so strong that she took a step forward before she recalled that time had taken its toll. She was no longer the girl who could touch him and find tenderness in his blue eyes—eyes that smoldered now in anger.

He hates me. The knowledge came to Victoria like a blow. She'd understood long ago that her pitiful rebellion had destroyed their friendship, that she'd asked from Ben something he'd regretted. Why else had he disappeared from her life without explanation? But why hate? And why after eight years should it be as fresh as yesterday? Victoria didn't understand, and despite the years, the look had the power to hurt. Still, she would not cower before it. Drawing one long, deep breath, she faced him squarely, with a proud and determined tilt of her head. As naturally as she could manage, she smiled up at him, ignoring his anger.

"You look wonderful, Ben. Time has been good to you." She was pleased that her voice was as usual, low and clear, with no trace of bravado.

"Why're you here? Why, after all this time, have you bothered to come back?" Ben ignored her efforts, his question lashing at her. Without actually moving, he seemed to brace himself for her answer.

Victoria stared at him, searching for some hint of the man she'd known. Did he no longer exist? Had he ever existed, except in the ardent imaginings of a love-starved girl?

"Answer me, Victoria. Now!" The rapier sharpness of his tone stabbed through her wandering thoughts.

This was all wrong. There was more in this man than she knew, something hidden. What had changed Ben into this unbending specter? Why did she see fear in him? Dear heaven, was Ben afraid of her? The thought was too much for her whirling mind to grasp. Confused, unable to reconcile past with present and suddenly far too weary to care, she knew only that she must answer as he demanded. Pushing a strand of hair from her face and grimacing in distaste at its limp dampness, she said tonelessly, "I was just passing through. I stopped because I wanted to see the castle."

"Why?"

"It was my home."

"Was it? Was it ever your home? Dammit! You didn't even bother to come back when your parents died."

"I would have! By the time I heard, weeks had passed. What was the need then? What could I have done?" She paused, rubbed her temple gingerly with her fingertips.

She had to tilt her head back to look at him. The dazzling light of the baking sun blinded her. A sweltering heat rose about her in distorting waves, and the headache that had threatened became a reality. With no warning her knees were shaking violently. In one crushing instant the throbbing discomfort progressed from annoying to vicious. Her vision blurred; her skin grew clammy. Victoria knew that she must sit down or disgrace herself by falling at his feet.

Could Ben walk away unconcerned, leaving her to lie in the mud? She searched his cold face and found her answer, and the pain in her head seemed to intensify.

"You're lying, Victoria!" In his anger he was totally unconscious of her distress. "The press made no secret of it."

"I didn't see the papers until it was far too late."

"I don't believe you."

"I . . ."

"Just couldn't be bothered," he finished for her, his voice stony, the words clipped.

"No! Damn you! It wasn't like—" She broke off shortly. Each new beat of her pulse brought a fresh wave of pain, and Victoria knew she could delay no longer. She must sit down. Now! Blindly, hands outstretched and fingers splayed, she fumbled her way to a small flat boulder. Thankfully, she sank down on it, drawing her knees up, burrowing her face in her folded arms.

Oblivious to her desperate state, Ben poured his wrath over her. "You must take me for a fool. First your own name is splashed over every newspaper rag in the country as they speculated about your disappearance. Then the most socially prominent people on the eastern coast die in a crash headlined in every village and city from Maine to Florida, and you expect me to believe you didn't know?" He added an ugly expletive under his breath, drawing a low moan from her.

She huddled in misery at his feet, enduring the low lash of his voice. One thing hadn't changed. The angrier Ben became, the softer he spoke. Despite the menace in his voice, she was grateful for the quiet. She raised her head, trying to focus on him, and by sheer willpower alone her tenuous control reasserted itself. "They were my parents, Ben. I loved them."

"Did you?" A look of loathing crossed his face, and he spoke more softly than ever. "Victoria, you're a selfish, heartless bitch. You've deserted everyone who ever loved you, even..." He stopped as if he'd said too much.

But Victoria was no longer listening. A cold, calming anger blanked out his sudden hesitancy. Reaching deeply within herself, she found a stubborn wisp of pride and strength that masked a growing weakness. She would allow nothing to destroy the remnants of her composure. Unflinchingly she met his brutality. "Don't judge me, Ben. You've no right."

"Don't I?" He raked her with a look that tarnished precious memories. "Then," he taunted, "who better than I?"

"None should judge." Her fingers curled into her palm, her nails cutting into it. Her voice carried the crack of a whip as she spoke to the blurred shadow he'd become. "Whatever I did, I had to do. I've spent eight years rebuilding my life. I've trained and worked in my chosen profession, and it was a good one. No one can make me the lesser for it." Despite her efforts, she weakened; her head drooped. "Not even you."

"From the look of you I'd hardly call it a successful life," he scoffed. "Do you need money? Is that why you're back? Certainly love would never be the enticement."

"No!" She defied the soft cruelty that made a mockery of all she'd salvaged from the destruction of her young life. Desperately she tried to rise, to face him and deny his unfair accusations, but she couldn't stand. Her shaky legs failed her, and she sank back to the hard stone. The fevered brightness of her gaze locked with his. Mutely, she shook her head in frustration and looked away.

She was small and defenseless curled on the stone there before him. For the first time her fragility penetrated the fog of fear that had gripped him at the gut-wrenching instant of recognition. Blinding scales dropped away. He saw the mottled skin that had once glowed with good health and a gaunt body that was no longer lush. The burnished gold of her hair had darkened and hung in wisps about her face. The hand that brushed back a stray lock had the tremor of age.

As quickly as it had come his rage died. Victoria was no longer the prodigal princess, a threat to his well-ordered world. She was a destitute woman.

"Are you ill?" he asked with a new gentleness.

"No," Victoria assured him in a voice that had regained its normal tone. "Just tired."

Was she truly just tired? she wondered. As she looked up at him, towering so unforgivingly over her, he seemed to weave and waver, yet he hadn't moved. She shook her head to clear it and firmly drew herself erect. Her pulse was strong, but a bit thready. She mustn't be ill. "I've come a long way, Ben. The heat's made me more tired than I expected."

"Where've you been, Victoria?" he asked. "How far have you come?"

Why wouldn't he stand still? Why couldn't she focus? A strange hollow laugh rang out. Belatedly she realized that it was she who laughed. Because she couldn't see him, Victoria didn't know that he flinched at its discord. Groggily, she remembered his question. Where had she been? Again the dry rasp of laughter ripped at her throat. "I've come a long way, Ben. I've come from Purgatory."

"Does that mean you were on the street?" He looked hopelessly into her glazed stare as he waited for her answer.

"On the street? Ah, you mean was I a prostitute? Very nearly, but that could hardly be called a profession of choice. Instead I went to Purgatory and became a witch doctor." She giggled again, and the torrent of her laughter reverberated painfully against the walls of her skull. The bright light made her eyes ache, so she closed them and lost herself in muddled thoughts.

"Victoria." Was that soft voice Ben's? Had he stopped being angry? "Victoria."

"¿Qué?" Her heavy lids opened reluctantly. Through a haze of confusion she saw a sparkling lake, not dusty streets; a castle instead of huts; and Ben's grave face instead of smiling natives. In an anguished moment of clarity she remembered. The streets, the huts, the kind faces of her brown-skinned friends had been left behind. There would be no more Purgatory. She would never again see that sardonically named plantation in South America. She was home. The weary princess nobody wanted had truly come home.

Pain bloomed in her head, sending shards of agony through her. She'd been mistaken. This was more than fatigue. She'd gambled and lost. It had begun. The fire that had destroyed all medical supplies in the village hospital was to claim one more victim. She had to leave. She had to get away while one last shred of strength remained. Victoria struggled to her feet and was elated when her legs held.

Summoning a dignity that conquered fatigue and confusion, she faced him. "If I could trouble you for a lift to the main road, I'll catch a ride there. Then I'll be gone from your life, Ben. You can forget you ever saw me."

"Dammit, Victoria! Are you insane? You can't—"

"All right." She bent to pick up her battered duffel. "If you'd rather, I'll walk."

"No! I didn't mean that. I'll take you, but you can't stand by the roadside and hitchhike like a common—"

"A common what?" She faced him wearily. "I hitched my way here. I'll leave the same way."

"Like hell you will!" He raked her with the sharp piercing look of his bleak eyes. "I may not like you, Victoria, or what you've done, but I wouldn't send a dog out like that. You're no fool. You know it's dangerous to ride with strangers. You could be raped, or worse. And heaven help me, I have enough on my conscience without that."

"I'll be fine, Ben. I've been taking care of myself far better than you realize for quite some time. You needn't worry." Victoria understood his allusion. Even in distress she couldn't allow him to blame himself for a night shared eight years ago. "Don't let your conscience be bothered about me. You've nothing to reproach yourself for. Now if you'll excuse me, I'll be on my way."

Shouldering her duffel with no word of goodbye, she started across the meadow. Her eyes ached with unshed tears. He'd asked her why she'd come. Now she knew. It was not the castle, or that this was home. She'd come hoping Ben had returned to Riverton and that she'd catch a glimpse of him.

"A mistake," she muttered under a labored breath. "An awful mistake. One truly can't go home again."

As she said it she turned—only slightly, but it was enough. He was standing as she'd left him. A fresh breeze ruffled his hair. A shaft of light seemed to surround him, and he was the friend she'd loved and lost.

"Goodbye, Ben," she whispered. Her hand rose in a hesitant, unfinished salute, and she moved away.

Ben gave no sign that he'd seen the tiny wave, but he missed nothing about her as she walked with a faltering step over the thick grass. Slender, hardly a shadow of herself and cloaked in mystery, she was still Victoria. It was insanity, but he couldn't let her go.

"Victoria!" His shout was only a low broken murmur lost in the pounding of his running footsteps. No matter what had gone before and no matter the consequences, to catch her, to keep her, if only for a little while, was the most important thing in his life. He could have one hour, then he'd send her on her way. Surely no harm could come from that.

"Victoria, wait." His hand on her shoulder drew her from her desperate concentration. Her fading strength almost broke at the new look of concern she saw in his face.

"You're exhausted. Come with me. Eat and rest, then I'll take you to the main road." He seemed almost to plead, his fingers moving in an absent caress over the prominent bones of her shoulder.

Victoria found herself drowning in eyes that were no longer cold but filled with a caring warmth. It frightened her more than the arctic aloofness had before. How could she leave him as she must when he looked at her like this?

"No," she protested. "It's going to be dark soon. I have to be getting on. There's something I must have."

"We both know that if you don't rest, you'll be going nowhere. I don't want to keep you here any more than you want to stay." He paused, looked at his watch, and a scowl darkened his face. "If I promise to take you wherever you choose to go, help you to get what it is you need, will you come? For just an hour, not a minute longer. You can rest, and Precious can give you a sandwich and something to drink."

Precious! At the sound of the endearment, her heart twisted in a dull, hopeless ache. Caroline, of course. She'd forgotten.

Why, in all her wildest dreams, had she never thought of Ben as married, perhaps with a family? Had she nurtured some secret hope that one day the impossible could come to pass? Must she always be the fool, even in her dreams? Precious—a strange endearment. Stranger yet from Ben.

With an effort she forced herself to address his concern. "It's kind of you to offer, but I mustn't intrude."

She had meant to decline gracefully, calling on the training of a lifetime, but he gave her no choice. Before she could say more, he lifted her into his arms, holding her close. "You're dead on your feet, and you know it. I doubt you could take another step, and I suspect you're weak from hunger. You look as if you haven't eaten for days. The least I can do, for my own peace of mind, is see that you have a decent meal."

"Not food. Must have..." Her whisper faded. She thought she spoke, but her lips only moved in pantomime.

Ben looked down at the woman in his arms. Delicately beautiful, fragile, yet in her he sensed a strength. He drew her closer, straining to hear the soundless words. "Never mind, princess. It can't be so important it won't wait. Rest. Then you'll be better."

When she would have struggled against his hold, his grip tightened. He brushed his lips against her hair and said grimly but gently, "Hush, Victoria. Rest. Please."

Victoria admitted defeat, accepting how right it felt to have his arms about her, to listen to the beat of his heart, to feel his muscles ripple under her cheek. Contentment and the even pace of his steps lulled her into oblivion. She was hardly aware when he set her easily into the passenger seat of a comfortable car. The deep snarl of the heavy motor was lost to her. Once voices from a great distance disturbed her stupor.

"Shall I close the gate now, Mr. Stockton?"

"Not just yet, George. I'll be leaving again within the hour. Then Mrs. Barton will be coming by later."

"With the young miss?"

"Yes." Ben was evasive, as if he were keeping the man from saying more. In her nebulous state between sleep and waking, she meant to think on it, but the soothing sway of the moving car soon wiped it from her mind. She heard no more, not even the dull thud of the door as Ben left the car and circled to her side. His hand at her cheek woke her.

"Victoria, you're home."

"Hmm?" She snuggled farther into the seat.

"You're exhausted, aren't you?" Ben muttered, more to himself than to her. He brushed a tendril of hair from her hot face as he leaned over her. "Where've you been, princess? What have the years done to you?" He stared at her, searching for an answer in her gaunt face.

"Fool!" He cursed himself in bitterness. "What does it matter? She'll be gone soon."

He slid his arms beneath her shoulders and knees and lifted her from the seat. In long strides he carried her to the carved door of a small, elegant house. Before he could touch the knob, the door swung open.

"Mr. Ben. I thought I heard your car. It's too early yet for Mrs. Barton." The huge mountain of a woman filled the doorway. She would've been intimidating, except that she had the kindest of faces. Her twinkling eyes fell on Victoria huddled in his arms. "My goodness! What have we here? Such a pretty thing. Here, give her to me. I'll see to her."

Ben smiled, thinking how like her it was to ask no questions. "It would seem I've taken up your habit of collecting strays. I found her down by the lake. She looked tired and starved, so I brought her home to you. Give her something to eat and drink and let her rest awhile. She'll be leaving before Mrs. Barton comes."

"Leaving! She'll do no such thing! Only over my dead body. From the looks of her, she needs more than a meal and few minutes of rest." Her beefy arms reached to take Victoria from him. "I'll just take her into the den."

"No!" Ben drew away from her seeking hands. "There's no need. I'll take her." As he turned his attention back to Victoria, he missed the spark of curiosity that had kindled in the watchful eyes.

"All right. You just get her settled on the sofa. I'll bring tea and some nice sandwiches along before you know it." She hovered by his side for a moment longer, her gnarled hand stroking the sweat-dampened hair from the sleeping woman's face. "She's the prettiest thing I ever saw, even so bedraggled."

"The sandwiches," Ben prompted.

"In a jiffy," she promised, spinning on startlingly small feet and walking in a rolling gait to the kitchen.

True to her word, she reappeared almost instantly. Ben had hardly put Victoria down on the sofa before she loomed over them like a protective mountain bearing gifts. "Do you think we should wake her? Seems to me that a body who sleeps like that needs rest more than they do food. Why don't I just put these away. We can put her upstairs in the spare bedroom next to yours. Then in the morning, when she's slept out her weariness, I'll fix her a nice, nourishing breakfast."

"She won't be here in the morning. She's leaving tonight." Ben glanced again at his watch. "Within the hour."

"You can't mean that!" the woman protested.

"I think I hear the teakettle whistling." He took the plate of sandwiches and turned firmly away. He said no more to the agitated woman, leaving her no choice but to do as he'd obliquely suggested. With his arm about Victoria's shoulders, he helped her to sit erect. "Here, princess, can you wake enough to take a bite or two of this? By the time you do, the tea should be here.''

Victoria's heavy lids fluttered open. Brown eyes that had looked at him with the afterglow of rapture shining in them settled in a solemn gaze on his face. Once Ben's arms would've ached to hold her. He would've drawn her to him and eased her hurt by making it his own. Even now, despite the years he'd spent hating her, desire stirred deeply within him and he wanted her. A part of him would always want her. But too many years, too many mistakes and too many unanswered questions stood like an impenetrable barrier between them.

"I can't." Victoria pushed his hand away as nausea rolled in the pit of her stomach. Her gaze shifted as recognition of familiar surroundings swept away the last groggy dregs of sleep. "What am I doing here? Why did you bring me to this place?"

"I live here," he answered, setting the plate aside. "I have for the past seven years."

"Here? In the guesthouse? But why?" In her surprise she pulled away from his supporting arm.

"At first some sort of caretaker was necessary. It wasn't wise to leave it unattended, and it seemed like a good place to..." He paused, and a guarded look flickered in his face as he continued carefully. "It seemed a good idea for someone to live here, so Precious and I rented the guesthouse and served as keepers of the castle."

"I see." She touched her lips with a dry tongue. "Who...who does it belong to?"

"It belongs to me now," Ben said.

"To you!" She sat starkly erect as shock obliterated the insidious fatigue that gnawed like a ravenous predator at her strength. It would be a short-lived reprieve. "How could that be? How could you afford it?" She looked at him in horror. "Why would you want it?"

"It's mine because I bought and paid for it. I can afford it because my own company has done quite well lately. In accordance with the merger, after the accident all the Mallory holdings were solely Carlos's. It took him less than a year to leach it dry and into bankruptcy. When the castle went on the market I could barely afford the rent for the guesthouse, and certainly not the buyer's price. I was lucky no one else bought it in the first years."

Ben saw the expression of horror frozen on her face. "What's the matter, princess?" His drawl was darkly sarcastic, the name a sneer. "Does it disturb you that a poor boy from the wrong side of town owns your castle?"

"No. No, of course not," she protested. "But why?"

"The reasons are personal."

In a flash of uncomfortable perception Victoria asked, "What other Mallory holdings are now Ben Stockton's?"

Ben hesitated as if he wouldn't answer, then shrugged diffidently. "Everything. The stock is worthless—Carlos saw to that—but the buildings are leased."

"It makes no sense." Victoria's eyes were wide in question, and her unease increased. "Why, Ben?"

"You're as repetitious as a broken record." His expressionless face revealed nothing. "My reasons are personal, Victoria."

"Is this some sort of revenge? Did my family do something to you? Is that why you left Riverton? Did you return for retribution?" She had no idea why she said it—it had been a shot in the dark—but as he paled and his expression grew colder, she knew she'd been right. She clasped her hand over her mouth as her horror mounted. "That's it, isn't it? God forgive us, Ben, what did we do to you?"

The silence seemed to coil about her, sucking her breath into its empty void. She was battered by the assault of his cruel appraisal, yet his voice was no more than a whisper of gentle deception. "Don't you know, Victoria?"

There was a devastating finality in his query. A question that was not question, expecting no answer. And she had none.

"Here you go—a nice, restoring cup of tea." Victoria's attention flew to the approaching woman, the largest she'd ever seen, easily more than six feet, and who knew how many pounds of solid muscle. There was not an ounce of fat on the raw-boned body which was capped by intricately coiled orange hair. She radiated a warmth that matched her size. Her dancing green eyes offered Victoria comfort or caring or whatever the younger woman might choose. And in a time of heart-sore confusion, when it was needed most, a friendship was born.

"Thank you, Precious." Ben took the tray from her as calmly as though their discussion had been of no more consequence than a pleasant chat.

Victoria's startled gaze flashed to Ben and back again to the woman. This was Precious?

Her curiosity was answered by a smile and a nod. "I'm Precious McGee, Mr. Ben's housekeeper."

"My pleasure, Miss McGee," Victoria responded, repeating by rote the lessons of her childhood as she tried once more to absorb the unexpected.

"Never Miss McGee! Just Precious." Precious cocked her head and inspected Victoria. "I have the strangest feeling you look like someone I know—"

"You're mistaken," Ben interrupted. "She's a drifter passing through. There's no reason she should seem familiar."

"Maybe not—" Precious was unconvinced "—but there's someone. I can't quite get a handle on it. It'll come to me, though. I know faces like I know the back of my hand."

"That's enough, Precious! I think you'd best go back to the kitchen, and our guest ought to finish her meal. I'll be taking her to catch a ride shortly."

"Surely you don't mean to allow that, Mr. Ben."

"Don't interfere." Ben ignored her look of astonishment, waiting until she turned with a puzzled look and left them. In her absence, the silence was intolerable as Ben and Victoria grew exquisitely aware of each other.

"She meant no harm," Victoria said at last.

"I know." Ben ruefully ran his fingers through his rumpled hair. "I'll apologize tomorrow. Maybe I'll even bring her flowers, if she hasn't quit by then."

"She won't quit. She thinks far too much of you."

"More than I deserve," Ben agreed as Victoria picked up her cup and rose to wander through the room, touching one remembered treasure after another. She paused before the fireplace, glancing at the blank wall that had held her portrait. He waited for some reaction. There was none.

She sipped absently from her cup and turned her back to the fireplace. "It's time I was going."

"Daddy, daddy!" The lively call preceded the clatter of scampering feet.

"No!" Ben lurched clumsily from his seat as a small, compact body topped by a mass of black curls catapulted into the room.

"Daddy," the child stopped before him, declaring with an emphatic shake of her head. "We simply have to find me a mommy."

"Oh, Lainie," Ben whispered hoarsely as he drew her into his arms.

Three

———

Victoria's cup hit the smooth marble of the hearth in a shattering crash. As she stared vacantly down at the blur it had become, man, woman and child stood frozen in the inertia of surprise. Then in the shocked stillness there was the sound of her stifled sob.

Slowly, as if caught in a nightmare, Victoria lifted one trembling hand to her face, pressing clumsy fingers against her eyelids in an effort to clear her vision. She sank to her knees and began to gather up each fragment with fierce care. As she scrabbled about, head bowed and shoulders hunched, the broken cup became the obsession of a mind that refused to function.

"Sweetheart." Ben's hands curled possessively about the small sturdy body of the child as he sought to divert her. "Why don't you run out to the kitchen and ask Precious to give you a glass of milk and some of the cookies she baked.''

"But—"

"Shh, shh." Ben tapped her lips lightly with a fingertip. "You just do as I say. I'll be in shortly, and you can tell me what happened to the movie."

The child nodded, sending a mass of ringlets tumbling about her face, and moved obediently from the circle of his arms. "But," she muttered dejectedly, more to herself than to Ben, "if I had a mommy of my own it wouldn't matter if Tommy Barton ate too much popcorn."

Victoria hadn't heard. She knew only that the throb in her head had once more become blindingly excruciating. Writhing on its jagged edge, she was beyond comprehension. She had no idea that her breath came in dry, keening moans, nor did she recognize Ben's inarticulate gasp of protest that came too late as a sweet voice spoke soothingly into her ear.

"Don't be scared, Daddy won't be mad. I promise. Sometimes I break things, but he never, ever yells at me."

Victoria stopped her frantic search for the elusive splinters buried in the carpet. For a moment that might have been an eternity she stared down at the bits of white and blue she held in her hands, then slowly she looked into the face of the child who knelt by her. From beneath tousled curls as black as Ben's, the little girl's golden brown eyes, like a mirror image, regarded her gravely.

Warmly, the steady contemplation, shatteringly familiar, touched Victoria, stripping away the protective shield from a part of her heart that had long been as empty as the grave. Innocently it laid bare an impossible hope. The insanity of it welled in her throat like the strangled whimper of a hurt animal. Her eyes were hot and dry as she crouched, shivering and afraid, on the floor by the fireplace.

At Victoria's distress, the straight brows of the little girl drew down in puzzlement, crinkling her forehead into a frown. Her eyes clouded in concern as her tongue worried her lower lip. As quickly as it had come, the frown brightened, replaced by the pleasure of the dawning of childlike understanding. "Don't worry," she said sympathetically. "If you're careful, you won't cut your finger, but if you do, Daddy'll kiss it and make it better." She looked up at Ben, and a snaggle-toothed grin transformed her face. "You will, won't you, Daddy?"

"Sweetheart, I'm not sure our guest would like that." Ben's strangled voice seemed to come from a great distance.

Victoria had forgotten he was there. When her eyes locked with his, she met full force the look of anger and fear she'd seen by the lake. Seared by its blazing heat, she looked away.

"Why don't you stop chattering like a magpie and go have the milk and cookies?" Ben suggested as he watched Victoria's averted face.

"They'll spoil my dinner." The threat was delivered with the playfulness of an old, comfortable argument.

"This time we'll make an exception. Now, scoot."

"Yes, sir." The obeisance was long and drawling, as full of mischief as of respect. After a pat for Victoria's shoulder, a kiss for Ben's cheek and a lighthearted giggle, she was gone in a flash of pink tennis shoes.

As an uneasy calm settled in the aftermath of the tiny whirlwind, Ben moved over to Victoria. "Put the

glass down on the hearth. Precious will see to it later."
He offered his hand. "You must be eager to be on
your way."

Mutely Victoria obeyed. Placing her cold, shaking
hand on his, she let him draw her to her feet. Like a
rag doll she waited, head down, body lifeless, drained
and more frightened than she'd ever been in her life.
Ben had begun to lead the way to the door when she
stumbled and would have fallen but for the support of
the arm of a tall chair. Helplessly she sank down into
it, as grateful for the rest as for its strength.

Ben turned back with an angry gesture, anxious to
take Victoria away, to put her from his life and have
done with this moment, which had brought near disaster. Yet for an instant, as he stared at her ravaged
body, he felt a flicker of hunger for the woman-child
she'd been. But it was only an instant, then the reali-
ties of today intruded on the lost dreams of yesterday.

"Come, Victoria," he said in an inflexible mono-
tone. "There's nothing left for you here."

She seemed beyond his voice, cataleptic in her concentration as she sat transfixed, her gaze intense, unwavering. An omen of dread fed his anger, destroying
his compassion and hunger.

"Who is she?"

Ben tensed, her small whisper plunged into him like
a knife, his dread a reality. Fingers convulsed, cutting
cruelly into the palms of his strong hands in a struggle for composure. "She's my daughter," he said
simply.

"Your daughter." She nodded, her eyes roving from
the arrogant line of his brow to the midnight hair that
tumbled over it, and then again to his eyes. Eyes as
blue as the sky that kissed a summer sea. "Yes, yes,"

she said in a slow, quivering breath. "Your daughter...and mine."

"No." His denial was harsh as he swung away, breaking contact, his shoulders heaving with the effort.

"You called her Lainie."

"You're mistaken."

"Lainie." The name flowed from her like a caress. "The name I gave her."

Ben recoiled, his powerful body warding off the inevitable. "She's only five years old and—"

"She's seven. She must be seven! Please don't lie." Bewilderment and a raw, primordial pain wove through the low, muted cry. "Please, Ben. Please don't lie."

The soft desperation in her plea reached him as nothing else. Finally he turned. Her face was lifted to his, her skin taut and ashen, her features chiseled. Like graven stone she waited in the false calm that skirted the edge of dementia. And in the mask of her face, only her eyes lived.

Ben recognized his defeat. "I suppose there's no point in denying it anymore," he said, resigned.

"Say it," she begged, grasping his wrist with a wild strength that belied her fragility. "Please say it."

For a moment Ben wondered if there was truly madness in the dark glitter of the eyes that clung to his. It was the only explanation for the latent hysteria that threatened. As the compelling gaze riveted his, he wanted to turn away, but she held him, refusing him release. Slowly, the truth, the affirmation she begged, was drawn inexorably from him.

"Lainie is my daughter. Conceived the night you came to me here." Nothing in the world could have stopped him from adding bitterly, "The child you gave away."

Her eyes closed, breaking the mesmeric stare as lashes lay like soot on ghostly cheeks. The manacle of her fingers loosened. As she hugged her arms closely about her, they clutched unconsciously at the fragile fabric of her blouse. At last her tears began—but not for his cruelty, for she had no recall of it. She knew only the joy of truth. She shed her tears for that truth and for old griefs that the heart is slow to relinquish. As hope touched the dark of her soul, the shadows fled, washed away by the salt of her tears.

"Conceived the night you came to me here." Eight words. With them he'd swept away the hurt of eight years and given her the gift of her child.

"Thank you."

The astonishing words were so low, so strangled, that Ben wasn't sure he heard. "Why are you thanking me? For what?"

"For wanting our child."

"For wanting her? Damn you, of course I wanted her." Ben's rage soared, slipping its tenuous leash, as old hurts crashed in on him. Yet even then, in the face of its futility and the travesty of his own conflicting emotions, he was reaching to a rockbed of cool reason. It was done. Not anger or hate or even love could change the past. For a time there was only silence as he accepted and waited for the storm to pass. Wearily he asked her, "Why, Victoria?"

"Why?" Ever so slowly, Victoria looked up from her incessant worrying of the frayed edge of her blouse. The single word brought a flood of memories, and beneath their assault a tormented, unprotected mind too sick to cope with its chaos slipped into the lonely, bitter void of the past.

"Dead..." she muttered indistinctly as she began to rock back and forth, her shivering body starkly erect. "Dead...told me...dead... Oh, God!" Her voice sank to a low cry. "Why?" Abruptly she grew still. Her dilated pupils, nearly obscuring the tiny rim of gold, were darkly vacant. As the fading light from the window struck them, there was no response. The gaze that settled on his face asked nothing, offered nothing, and Ben stood stunned by the frightening feeling that suddenly no one was there.

"I'm sorry, Victoria. I don't understand." He didn't realize that he spoke with an aching gentleness. "Why did you give our baby away?"

"Oh, Ben." She spoke in an eerie chant, the sing-song voice that of the young Victoria. "You know there's no baby. There never will be. Poor baby. Nobody wanted her. Not Mother, not Father, not Carlos. Only me. I wanted her. I tried...but it wasn't enough. Nobody loved the poor baby princess, so she died." Finally something stirred in the dark well of her eyes. An anguish that was worse than the emptiness. "Our baby died, Ben."

Ben knew then that what he saw was the madness of a chilling hysteria and that what he heard was the truth as she believed it. While he struggled to absorb that truth, Victoria shivered and looked away.

"I must go," she said in the same ghastly chant. Gracelessly grasping the chair for support, she stood, reeling once, drunkenly. Placing one foot carefully in front of the other in slow, deliberate steps, she left the room. Her footsteps were barely more than a whisper on the polished parquetry of the hallway, but in them Ben heard again the sound of goodbye.

She was leaving, vanishing from his life. Taking with her the answers to old questions that haunted, the resolution of new mysteries that would torment. For one hour she'd come into his life, tearing away the curtain of the past, rewriting history. Changed yet unchanged, she'd been magnificent. Frail and weary but still strong, dusty and travel-worn but unconsciously elegant, she was the princess. Angles and shadows had made her no less lovely. Ben admitted now that beneath the fear and anger and the hidden guilt that plagued him, the throb of desire prevailed. In his turmoil of questions and mysteries, anger and fear, guilt and desire, Ben realized that mad or not, she held the key to his life. *I can't let her go!*

"Victoria." He wasn't surprised when she continued to move ponderously down the hallway toward the door as if she hadn't heard. He was sure she hadn't as he walked quickly after her. She'd heard very little and understood less since the moment he'd called Lainie's name.

"Victoria!" He caught her wrist and turned her toward him. Cupping her face in his hands, he lifted her glazed eyes to his. They held no trace of recognition. "Good grief! You're burning with fever. No wonder you're half out of your head with shock. Why didn't you tell me you were ill? Dammit!" The low, angry curse was meant for himself. "Why should you have to tell me the obvious?"

He swung her into his arms, cradling her head against his chest as it dropped heavily against him. She was at last unconscious. "Precious!" There was frantic distress in his cry. "Come here. I need you."

Two pairs of running footsteps danced and thudded from the kitchen into the hall and stopped short.

"Land o' Goshen! I knew she was sick! The very idea that she could stand on the roadside and thumb! Thumb, mind you, like a hippie or a yippie or whatever they're called." As she grumbled, Precious was examining Victoria, who lay flushed and restless in Ben's arms. "Now maybe you'll listen to me and put her in the spare bedroom like I said. Or better yet, in the extra bed in my room, where I can look after her."

"No. I'll put her in the spare bedroom." He stepped on to the staircase and looked back at Precious. "Call Dr. Jim, then get me what she needs. Cool compresses or whatever, and show me what to do. I'll take care of her."

"Yes, Mr. Ben," Precious answered briskly, offering no argument. "You take her on up to bed. I'll be up in a minute. We're going to have to sponge her in cool water and alcohol to get her fever down." She looked down at the frightened child. "Lainie, don't you be scared. We're going to make the pretty lady all better."

"Like Daddy does with his kisses?"

Precious waited as Ben disappeared beyond the landing of the stairs. She looked absently after him for a moment, then swung her large bulk swiftly to stare hard at the bare wall that stretched emptily above the mantel. "Well, glory be!"

With a cracking of stiff knees and turbulent sway of her voluminous skirts, she knelt before the child. Her kind regard considered every feature, hair and brows as black as coal, golden brown eyes and a sweet generous mouth, smooth and tawny cheeks that dimpled when she smiled.

"Well, glory be and at last the blind shall see," she said again as she smiled and drew Lainie into her arms, rocking her against huge breasts. A low, pleased chuckle rumbled in her throat, setting the soft flesh quivering beneath Lainie's cheek. "Now that you mention it, child, I think your daddy's kisses could go a long way toward making her well.

"But," she panted in the effort of rising, "for now I guess we'd better use other methods. Run and get those new cloths from the linen closet. I'll get the basin and the alcohol. Once I call Dr. Jim and show your daddy what he must do, I'd best be putting you to bed, young lady."

"Precious!"

"Don't you Precious me in that pitiful voice. No complaining allowed. Hurry, your daddy's waiting."

Ben had missed the exchange. He'd carried the slight weight of his burden up the remaining stairs and shouldered his way into the spare room. He crossed quickly to the bed, awkward in his haste, and threw back the smartly tailored coverlet, heedless when it slipped and slithered to the floor. Carefully he laid Victoria on the bed.

As he leaned over her, memories of another room, another time, were a throbbing ache in his heart. His expression was as black as storm clouds as he stroked her cheek with the back of his hand. "What happened, princess? Where did we go wrong so long ago? Why didn't you come to me? Didn't you believe that I would want you and our baby? Were you too young to realize I loved you?"

There was no answer. He expected none. He sat by her beside, waiting as seconds dragged slowly into minutes that could have been hours. Victoria stirred, muttering unintelligibly. Ben was alarmed, sure she was in pain and angry at his own helplessness. "Where the hell is Jim?" he muttered. "Why doesn't he come?"

"Because he's a man, not a magician," Precious said from behind him. "Land o' Goshen, Mr. Ben. He can't sprout wings and fly. He said he'd be here as soon as he could.'' She moved to his side, and despite her unruffled manner, Ben saw there was worry in the pinched line of her mouth. Precious would worry for the young woman who tossed restlessly, twisting the sheet he'd drawn over her into a tangle; and she would worry for him, a quiet man not given to profanity, whose cursing was a measure of his agitation. When she placed her hand on his shoulder, he drew a small comfort from it.

"Are you sure he was coming directly here?" Ben asked, soothed a bit by her kindliness.

The ringing of the doorbell interrupted her answer. Precious turned with surprising speed and ran from the room. Soon Ben heard the cadence of hushed greetings and low conversations, then muffled treads climbed the stairs. Why was it, he wondered, that sickness and death brought with it the pall of stifling, smothering silence?

"Ben." A huge hand on his shoulder broke into his tortured thought. He lifted a blank face toward the man whose tranquility was a contradiction of his gigantic stature. "You look tired. Why don't you rest a minute."

"I can't leave her, Jim."

"Yes, you can. Go have a cup of coffee, or kiss your daughter good-night. At this minute Victoria needs me more than she does you. Go, Ben," the doctor urged, promising, "I'll take care of her."

Ben nodded tiredly, succumbing to the wisdom of a trusted friend, and rose from his vigil. Jim, a bearlike man with a mane of silver and eyes to match, slid into his place. Not a flicker of surprise showed on his tired, lined face as he placed his hand at the pulse at Victoria's throat. "Poor little Vicky, what kept you away so long?"

Ben paused at the door. He'd taken one step back toward the bed when Jim growled gruffly, without looking up from his task, "Go have that cup of coffee, Ben. And kiss your daughter twice. Once for me. By the time you have, I'll be finished here. We'll talk then."

Jim was as good as his word. He dispatched his duties efficiently, compassionately, even lovingly, in a matter of minutes. Minutes that in the crawl of time were, again, endless for those who waited. Ben had checked on a fretfully sleeping Lainie and was sitting in the den, staring down distractedly at a neglected cup of coffee, when the physician joined him.

"Jim!" Ben drew himself from his absorption. "Should we leave Victoria alone? He was in the act of rising when Jim stopped him with a commanding gesture.

"She'll be all right for a while. I gave her something to help her rest." Jim sampled the steaming brew Precious set before him. "Ahh. This is good."

Ben broke into the familiar monologue about Precious's coffee. "How is she now? What's wrong with her?"

"Well, I'd say she's a pretty sick young woman, but I doubt there's any real danger." He sipped again from his cup and smiled at Precious. "I do believe this is your best yet, my dear."

"Jim," Ben said through gritted teeth, "I'm glad you like the coffee. Precious is glad you like it. I'll have her make you a gallon. Two! But right now I want to know what's wrong with Victoria." He liked Jim and understood his easy ways, but at the moment he had no patience with this gentle giant. Instead he wanted to lash out, to hit something and batter away his worry.

With an insight gained from the long years of their friendship, Jim recognized the turmoil that clawed at Ben's frantic mind and countered the younger man's frustration with deliberate honesty. "I can't give you an answer for sure, Ben."

"Why the devil not? You're an astute diagnostician. There's not much that gets by you."

"I'd say it's because I suspect this is not your common garden-variety illness. And certainly not something we find around here."

"What do you mean?" Tension carved deep brackets about Ben's mouth. "What do you think it is?"

"Malaria."

"Malaria!" Brown liquid splashed over the rim of Ben's cup. He stared at it for an instant, then carefully set it down. "There are medications that prevent it, aren't there?"

"Yes."

"Then why didn't she take one?"

"That's something only Vicky can answer."

"Where on earth could she have contracted it?"

"Any tropical country, a jungle, a rain forest."

"Jungle!" A recollection of disjointed ramblings he'd discounted as nonsense blazed across Ben's thoughts. "Jim, Victoria said some wild things about Purgatory and witch doctors. At the time I paid no attention. I won't go into my reasons, but I thought she said it to taunt me. Is it possible she was in a jungle?"

"Stranger things have happened. I imagine she got those scars on her hands and arms at this Purgatory, too." Jim said mildly, appearing as undisturbed as ever. He set his cup down with reluctance and stood.

An image that sickened rose from Ben's subconscious. He'd seen without seeing the raw and newly healed tissue on sun-darkened fingers that had clasped his wrist in pleading anguish. Wounds as mysterious as they were horrible, one more unanswered question. The steady hand he ran through his hair betrayed none of the bewilderment that clouded his face.

"I'd best be getting on," Jim said. "I'd like to get some blood samples to the lab for confirmation. I'm pretty sure about this, but I'd like these tests to back me up." He gestured again for Ben to remain seated. "On my way out I'll explain to Precious what I'd like you to do for Victoria."

Ben watched as the only man he knew who made Precious look small followed her from the room. He picked his cup up from a table, grimaced and set it down. His gaze again returned to the empty wall before him, searching it as if to make her likeness appear.

"Princess," he asked aloud of no one, "where've you been? What's happened to you?"

Crisp sheets that smelled of sunshine and lavender were cool to her burning body. The ache in her head was eased by the assuasive pressure of a moist cloth. Gentle fingers massaged her temples, and her tiredness seemed to drain away. Each time the cloth grew warm it was taken away and then replaced by a fresher, cooler one. It was bliss to lie there, to sink further and further into contentment. The pleasures of being cared for and comforted wove a magic chrysalis about her. Perhaps...after she rested...she could rise and become a beautiful butterfly.

"A yellow butterfly," Victoria muttered through lips that had begun to crack from fever.

"What's she saying, Precious? Why is she talking about butterflies?" Ben's fatigue from long hours by Victoria's bedside was evident in the rusty, unused quality of his voice.

"Shh, Mr. Ben," Precious soothed him. "She doesn't know what she's saying. The fever has her talking confusion. Most likely she's dreaming about butterflies. It's doubtful she'll remember when she wakes up."

"She's been like this for hours. Shouldn't she be better by now? Maybe we should call Jim back."

"Now, you heard Doc, same as I did. She's in no immediate danger, and it'll take days for this to run its course. We're doing all we can for now by keeping her fresh and cooling down her fever." Precious waited while Ben changed the cloth that lay over Victoria's forehead. "Why don't you let me do that. Lainie's sleeping poorly tonight. One of us should check on her."

"You go. I'm fine here."

"Maybe you should stretch out on your bed for a few hours. You can open the adjoining door and I can call you if I need you," Precious persisted.

"I said no." He didn't look away from the flushed face on the pillow. He expected no more dissension, certain Precious was wise enough to know when an argument was useless. Her years with him had taught her he was reasonable to a point. Beyond that he couldn't be moved.

His hand slipped beneath Victoria's where it was curled, clawlike, on the sheet. He winced as her scarred fingers tightened over his.

"Her fever's rising." Precious prudently tried a new approach. "The medication Jim gave her isn't working as it should. She should be sponged down."

"I know." He smoothed back Victoria's hair as he had endlessly through the evening.

"I'll get my supplies so I can begin."

"I can do it."

"Maybe you should let me."

"I'll do it, Precious. I have to."

Four

———

A pan of water flanked by a stack of clean towels sat on the bedside table. He had struck a bargain with Precious; he would rest tomorrow. Reluctantly she'd gathered the linen, repeated his instructions and taken herself to bed. Ben was alone with Victoria.

A small shaded lamp filled the room with muted light, washing lines and drabness away. With her hair strewn over the pillow, Ben could almost imagine this was the Victoria of the past, that the lost, lonely years had never been. A quick, hard spasm seized her. Her face twisted in pain and her frail body thrashed, sending the sheet into greater tangle. He touched her burning forehead.

Jim's medication had run its course. Victoria must be sponged to cool her fever. His hand rested against the pristine white towel; the cool water waited in a small basin. He knew he must begin. But he was reluctant to slip the sheet from her naked body, reluctant to put his hands on the curves and hollows that had lived in his memory. It seemed an obscene invasion to touch her without her knowledge.

"Forgive me, princess. I have to." He lifted the towel and dipped it into the water. He wasn't sure he heard it, that small, sobbing cry, yet he stopped, waiting, unbelieving. Then he heard it again.

"I hurt."

Her unblinking eyes stared harshly through him. But Ben only cared that she was conscious. It was a good sign. He leaned nearer to comfort her. "I know you hurt, but you'll be better soon. I promise."

"I hurt, Mommy. I cut my knee." Her face contorted in terror and the childish voice grew shrill. As the plaintive wail dwindled to a whimper, Ben turned to ice. Victoria was in a time and place he couldn't go.

"Blood, Mommy, there's blood!" Victoria shivered. Her head was flung back, then forward. Terror left her; her face screwed into a duplicate of youthful remorse. Her voice sank to a humble plea. "I'm sorry, Mother. I didn't mean to stain your dress. I'm sorry...sorry...sorry..."

"Ahh, no," Ben cried into the sudden void. He remembered a wicked scar on a beautiful slender leg, one he'd regretted even as he'd kissed it. Now he saw an even deeper wound, one left by a mother more concerned with the perfection of her dress than in offering solace to a frightened child.

There was more. Stunned, he sat immobile through the muttering of a child who'd been a possession, tolerated only as a reflection of the parent. He heard it time after time, the desperate seeking of love through approval, countered by the expectation of perfection. He understood, at last, the tractable and pliant daughter who could marry the man her father had decreed.

In all the years, he'd never known, never guessed. *"I didn't know you were such an accomplished actress,"* he'd said. *"I've been acting all my life"* had been her reply. Simple words that now assumed a clearer yet more complex meaning and exposed the emotional abuse she'd kept hidden. Even from him.

Victoria's body shuddered, her sweat-soaked hair tangled, her respiration grew quick and shallow and still she rambled. Ben realized he could delay no longer. With a cool towel he began to stroke her face and neck. His expression was bleak, but his hand was steady when he slipped the sheet from her. In careful, soothing circles, he cooled her body. As the heat of her fever scorched away the moisture, he turned patiently for fresh towels. And all the while he tried not to see; he didn't want to hear.

The nightmare had only begun. At some unnamed hour he began to walk with her through her life. She had laughed about her Purgatory; he had found his.

"No, Mother. Please, no. Not abortion!"

The fresh cloth slipped from Ben's nerveless fingers.

"Please don't make me. Yes, yes, I'll tell Carlos. I'll ask him." Tears trickled across her cheek, blending with beads of perspiration. A broken sob corded her throat.

Ben sat helpless, grave faced, the cloth forgotten as he listened to her plead for the life of their unborn child.

"No, please, no." Her head tossed incessantly from side to side, her hair plastered by sweat and tears to her face. "I'll go away. I won't disgrace you. I won't tell anyone, not anyone. I'll give my baby up, but please,

please, don't make me kill it." The frantic thrashing of her body ceased. The calm of deadly panic caught at her, shredding her. A low keening moan, raggedly inhuman, tore from her, rising to a desperate scream. "Please don't make me kill my baby!"

As he took her into his arms, Ben didn't know there was blood welling from the cut of his bitten lip. As he rocked her in his embrace, the only pain he knew was hers as she fought a terrible battle. With his cheek resting against her hair, his eyes fixed on the darkened clouds that gathered on the horizon, he went with her step by step through the lonely, frightening months that followed. He didn't know it was his tears that bathed her as he fled with her from the death of their little girl.

Immersed in the horror, Ben had no idea how long it was before he realized Victoria had grown still. Her delirium had subsided, her temperature cooled and her restlessness abated. She was peaceful in mind and body. For the first time in hours she slept a natural sleep. Carefully he released her, leaning her back onto the tumbled bed. Slipping his arms slowly from beneath her, he rose. He made no noise, yet something penetrated her slumber.

"Help me."

"I'm here. I'll help you." He dropped to his knees by the bed.

"Too late. Nobody can help. My baby's dead."

"No, princess. When you're better you'll remember, and someday, together, we'll find a way to understand what happened." Her unfocused gaze told him that she was caught in the web of the past, that his promise held no meaning. He looked down at the angular lines of her body, over breasts that were full even in her thinness, down the prominent ridges of her ribs, to the concave hollow of her belly. Tiny striations that gleamed pale in the low light marred the perfection of her skin. They were the mark of courage; to him they were beautiful.

His hand was gentle as he laid it where his child had once been cradled. How lovely she must've been in the rich fruition of their loving. Of all his regrets, that he'd never seen her with child—his child—brought an ache that was most bittersweet.

"Someday," he murmured as his lips touched where his hand had lain.

Slowly, Ben stood and crossed the room. From a stack he took two sheets. One he folded and smoothed to slip beneath Victoria's head. He drew the second over her. When he'd finished, after one glance to reassure himself that she slept restfully, he sank to the floor at her side. As he leaned there wearily, the back of his hair was dark against the white sheet. He closed his eyes only to ease their sting, but tensions of a long day and a longer night claimed their reckoning.

Victoria stirred. Her hand crept over the cover; her disfigured fingers burrowed into the thickness of the sleeping man's hair. A smile eased the gaunt lines of her lips.

For days, with Precious's help, Ben battled her fever and delirium. Victoria's story poured out again and again, and from the calm acceptance on Precious's face, Ben knew she'd long connected the discarded portrait to Victoria, and Victoria to Lainie. Her suspicions were never discussed. There was no need. As they shared the bedside vigil, sponging, medicating, soothing, one name was strangely missing from Victoria's rambling. From childhood through tragedy

to her days in the jungle, Ben might never have existed.

As they worked together, Precious cheerful and
optimistic, Ben grim and determined, Jim was
constantly in attendance, guiding them. In the background, forbidden the sickroom, Lainie moved like a
wraith, big-eyed and unnaturally subdued.

In the late afternoon of the fourth day, Victoria's
fever broke for the last time.

It was day. She could tell by the brightness that
weighted her eyelids. Instead of the chatter of natives
punctuated by the shrieking of birds, she was surrounded by a relative serenity. Then she recognized
that the low hum overhead was a fan, not the rustle of
thatch.

Puzzled, she opened her eyes a fraction, letting the
light seep in, by habit delaying the unrelenting assault
of the tropic sun. Through a fringe of lashes she saw
long legs molded by khaki. Surprised by the shaded
light, she allowed her lids to drift open another fraction. A lean torso and broad back covered by a tailored, cream-colored shirt filled her vision. Her eyes
widened then, amazed at the man who stood at the
window, staring into the distance. "Ben?"

With the clean grace of a man who'd fought his way
out of squalor into the ranks of the intelligentsia and
to corporate success with great athletic ability, Ben
swung away from the window and from the patch of
bright light that sprinkled his hair with black dia-
monds. As he stepped out of the brilliance into the
umbra of the room, the lazy whirl of the ceiling fan
teased a damp lock and he pushed it absentmindedly
from his forehead. His clothing was crisp and fresh,
but despite a cool shower, his body was not. The hours

of watching and waiting had lined his face with fatigue; the emotional roller coaster he'd ridden had drawn him to a fine edge.

In the half light he watched her struggle with reality as he'd watched for four days while she'd struggled from the depths of the hell of illness. He'd watched and he'd listened. In her ramblings she'd swept away the hate he'd harbored and resolved the haunting guilt. In the darkest hours when she'd slept the sleep of the exhausted, he'd at last faced the guilt and examined it. He knew now that he hadn't deserted her, that his presence in Riverton would've changed nothing. Even in her extremity she wouldn't have come to him. She hadn't called his name.

She hadn't wanted him then, but she would. He would see to it. She would want him as he wanted her. For himself and for Lainie. Victoria would be a part of the heritage he was building for his daughter. Their daughter.

"Ben?" she said again, disbelievingly.

"In the flesh," he said, and the somber lines of his face softened into a teasing smile as he stepped closer. "It's about time you stopped malingering and woke up."

"But how? Where? When..."

"Whoa. Take it easy. It'll all come back to you."

Victoria drew her brows down, concentrating with all her might. "The lake! We met at the lake."

"That's right," he encouraged her.

"How did I get here?"

"I brought you."

"Why?"

"You were ill."

Victoria rubbed her forehead distractedly. "I remember. I was dizzy. Surely that was no cause to bring me here and put me in bed. It would've passed in an hour or so.''

''I rather doubt it, princess. It's been four days. A bit more than a little dizziness, wouldn't you say?''

''Malaria.''

Ben nodded in unnecessary affirmation.

''I feel so stupid. I remember the lake. After that there's nothing. I've lost four complete days!''

''There's no hurry. If you're feeling up to it, why don't I run you a warm bath. Then, when you're through, I'll take you down to the garden and we'll talk.''

Victoria touched her hair and found it matted and stiff. ''A bath and a shampoo would be heaven.''

''One bath coming up.''

She waited as he moved with a light step to the bath. A cabinet door opened, then shut. The taps were turned and the rush of water became a muffled drone. The subtle fragrance of jasmine wafted through the room. Then Ben was back. Casually folding back the sleeves of his shirt, he advanced toward her.

She realized his intent, and her eyes widened in alarm. She'd already discovered, to her dismay, that beneath the thin protection of the sheet she was naked. ''No.'' She held her hand toward him, palm forward. ''I . . . I don't have on a nightgown.''

''I know that. With your tossing and turning and sweating, a gown was a nuisance.'' He didn't slow his deliberate pace as he finished with his sleeves.

''I can do it myself,'' she insisted.

''I don't think you realize just how sick you've been.'' He stopped, his hands on his hips, and waited patiently.

With a flash of pride on her face and a determined tilt to her chin, she accepted her own challenge.

Clutching the sheet to her breasts, she edged to the bedside and let her legs fall heavily over the side. Planting her feet firmly on the carpet, she tried to rise. Once, twice, a third time, she made the effort. Each time, her trembling knees betrayed her. Finally, weak with exertion, she looked mutely at him.

His look was grim with worry. "You're an independent little thing, aren't you?"

Before she could answer, he was towering over her, first looping a length of ribbon in the tangle of her hair, then, with gentle care, pulling the covering from her. "Stop!" Victoria muttered. "There's no need to do that. If you'll just help me to get to the bathroom, I can manage."

"You can't." He calmly continued to slip the fabric from her grasp. "And there's no need to drag this with us."

He was right, she admitted; she couldn't. And to argue at this point was foolish, as foolish as clinging to the sheet as if it were her lifeline. Slowly she relinquished her hold and let it slip completely away. Immediately, with one arm hard at her back, the other slipped beneath her knees, Ben scooped her up in a smooth, easy motion. At the touch of his gaze, a blush painted a hint of color over her cheeks.

Ben laughed softly. "You're too stubborn for your own good, and you're absolutely beautiful when you blush. You shouldn't blush, you know, I've seen your body. I've made love to you. I've spent the past few days bathing you. Now I'm going to bathe you again. And—" he sobered as he leaned near, his lips almost touching her, his breath a caress against her skin "—someday soon I'll make love to you again.

"Here you go," he continued casually, ignoring her sharply indrawn breath as he slid her into the water amid a drift of soap bubbles, then turned off the taps. With his arms folded over his chest, he asked, ''Now, would you like to soak, or would you rather we washed your hair?''

''I'll soak for a bit. Then I can wash my hair myself. You mustn't bother.'' She slipped farther under the fragrant fluff that tickled her breasts.

''No bother,'' he said absently, distracted by the sight of a dusky-tipped nipple as a spangled bubble clung in momentary quiescence, then drifted away.

Victoria followed the direction of his interest, flushed again and slid lower into the water. Her sudden move set the water to churning and a wave of jasmine-scented soap covered her chin.

''Careful,'' he warned, regaining his equilibrium. ''If you get any deeper into that tub, I'll have to get you a diving mask.'' With his hands resting on his hips, he watched her, smiling softly.

The quirk of his lips, the touch of his eyes, sent spirals of sweet fire through her. He disturbed her in a way she didn't understand. Nudity had been natural on the plantation. She'd grown comfortable with it and had even learned to relish the glorious freedom of swimming in surf or stream dressed in no more than a minuscule loincloth. Yet here, when she was confined by the trappings of civilization, this man's gentle scrutiny provoked a vague restlessness.

In her discomposure Victoria took refuge in irritation. She frowned at him, wishing he weren't so vitally, excitingly masculine. ''Are you going to hang about and spoil my lovely soak?''

''Wouldn't think of if. If you promise not to fall asleep and suffocate yourself in that fragrant fog, I'll go down to the kitchen.'' He ignored her protest. ''I know your stomach's not ready for a meal, but a little of Precious's beef tea and some toast should go a way toward building strength."

"Beef tea?" she said weakly.

"Yes." He chuckled at her expression of dismay. "But don't worry, it's not nearly as bad as it sounds. In fact, it's quite good, and Precious swears by its restorative powers. Now—" he assumed an attitude that precluded argument "—give me your promise."

"I promise," she agreed wearily.

"What do you promise?"

She looked at him blankly, confused by the long days of illness. Exasperated, she waved a hand at him, strewing bubbles in its wake and inadvertently exposing a rose-tipped breast for his covert admiration. "I can't remember exactly."

"Careful, princess." One brow lifted in amusement as he teased, "You could get yourself into a whole lot of trouble that way. One thing I said was that we would make love."

In the second it took for her befuddled brain to absorb the import, he spun on his heel. The door shut at his back, but not before she heard his quietly added "Very soon."

Victoria sat bolt upright, unmindful of the soapy water that splashed onto the floor. Her mouth opened in shocked surprise as her gaze locked on the empty space Ben had occupied. Did he tease, or did he promise?

"He's teasing." She willed herself to accept the least unsettling answer, the one that would require no probing of feelings long put aside or of new emotions that lay in wait in the deep center of herself. "Of course he is!"

Is he? Her mind asked disobediently.

"Don't be ridiculous, Missy," she chided herself sternly, using the name she'd grown accustomed to over the past years. "With that devilish smile, what else could it have been? Anyway, the age for girlish imaginings is long past." Slowly, sighing softly, she leaned back. After a time the sad, lost look faded from her face as she succumbed to the magic of the water.

She had meant only to soak for a while to relieve the tightness of her muscles and the bone-deep ache of weariness. Then she would scrub the stench of malaria from her skin and her hair. Ben had called her beautiful. She knew it was no longer true, but at least she could be clean and refreshed and waiting in her room when he returned.

But she hadn't reckoned with the languor that would come stealing over her. Her hair spilling from the ribbon and falling about her shoulders woke her. Ben knelt by the tub, armed with a bottle of shampoo and a fluffy towel. He smiled as he scolded. "Napping, princess? And after you promised."

"Mmm." She was too contented to rise to his banter.

"Precious meant to do this when she got back from town. But I'd been hovering there at your bedside for hours, staring at you, wishing you awake so that I could." He scooped up a sponge floating near her bent knee and ran it slowly over her shoulders and her back.

His hands glided over her to the taut muscles of her neck as her head drooped forward. Fingers that were strong but sensitive searched and probed and eased the knotted muscles. Tirelessly he stroked her tawny skin until her contentment deepened and the last stubborn tension drained away. Then, at last, the delicious massage was complete.

"Lean back now," Ben said huskily. "Just a bit."

Victoria meekly did as he asked and fell further captive to his ministrations. The sponge was moist against her cheeks and water trailed down her body. He washed the gritty residue from her shoulders and then, with exquisite care, he bathed her breasts. Her eyes closed as she murmured a dulcet sigh of pleasure, and she missed his searching look lingering on her upturned face.

There was a practiced ease about him as he applied himself to his appointed task. She marveled at the rightness of the feel of his hands on her body and wondered at his skill. Then, for a time, she relinquished herself with lazy abandon into his care. Before she knew it she was bathed and shampooed.

"All done." He tossed the sponge aside. "If we don't get you out of there soon, you're going to turn into a mermaid—a skinny mermaid. Come, princess, I'll dry you."

"No!" She was being foolish again and she knew it. The soapy translucence of the water had done little to hinder the quest of his marauding inspection, but the thought of his hands on her body without its protection disturbed her.

"Don't say you can do it yourself. You've already proved you can't. It's more than you can manage to stand, much less expend the energy it would take to dry yourself. So for now, stop fighting it and let me do the work." His arms slid under her, and he lifted her in a fragrant cascade.

"Your shirt," she protested belatedly. "You've gotten your sleeves all wet."

"They'll dry," he said with a strange matter-of-factness as he deposited her on the carpeted floor. He steadied her with one hand and pulled the towel from its folds with the other. His glance flickered over her, and something altered, intensified. "Hardly more than a mere scrap of yourself, and yet you're beautiful."

"I'm not."

"More beautiful than you know."

He had told her she was beautiful before, but this time there was something different in his tone. She had no time to seek out the answers before the huge towel enveloped her. He dried her with an unhurried care, as if she might break. By the time he tossed the towel aside, she was trembling with a weakness that had little to do with illness.

From a hook at the back of the door, he snagged an oversize shirt. He slipped her into it, chuckling at the long, flapping sleeves and teasing about the sexy show of leg beneath the tails. Then, properly buttoned and demure, she was seated before a dressing table. As carefully and gently as a lover, he began to brush her hair, working free the snarls, stroking and smoothing each strand into place.

Once, when his fingers lingered on the fluttering pulse at her throat, she felt a need to see his face, but his reflected expression was bland. Beneath the dark fall of his unruly hair he was heavy-lidded, his brow furled with the creases of concentration, his attention solely on his chore. A veil of disappointment shadowed her face. The caress had been in her mind, not in his touch.

Still she watched him, admitting her compulsion to look at him unfettered and unsuspected, to devour him. It was Ben who was beautiful. There was rugged elegance in his strength as the muscles of his shoulders and arms rippled at every sensual move. The sheer masculinity of him suffused her with untroubled pleasure, while the rhythmic pull of the brush through her hair mesmerized. Soon she drifted into a drowsiness that emptied her mind of thought.

"There," he said into the peaceful hush. He laid the brush aside, placed his hands on her shoulders and leaned to touch the top of her head with his lips. "Pretty as a picture. Are you ready for food?"

"Suddenly, I am. I..." As he turned her to face him her eyes traveled over and back again to a basket of unmistakable clutter. "I..." She faltered again, then clapped her hand to her lips. The pretty flush faded from her cheeks, leaving them stark white against the darkness of her disfigured fingers. The face she lifted to Ben was bewildered.

"Come with me, princess." Ben stroked her cheek, delaying the inevitable until they were in more comfortable surroundings. "Let's give the flowers in the garden some competition." He lifted her into his arms, aware that her bones were almost fleshless, and carried her down the stairs and to the terrace that overlooked the garden.

"Comfortable?" He adjusted her chair, chose a seat across from her, then from a warming tray he took toast and the threatened beef tea.

"I'm fine." Victoria looked down at the food before her with an appetite that had flown.

"You remember, don't you?" His hand covered hers as it lay nervelessly on the table. "You saw Lainie's bath toys and remembered. Were you afraid that you'd dreamed it? Were you afraid to believe?"

A silent sob rose, constricting her throat, and Victoria could only nod, but her heart was in her brimming eyes.

"Perhaps she's a miracle, but she's not a dream, you know," he said softly, his thumb moving over the tender skin of her wrist. "Lainie's a very lively and happy reality."

"How can it be?" she asked numbly. "How? I thought...I promised... Oh God, I promised. You never knew."

"No, I didn't, did I?" In spite of himself, the old resentment surfaced with its wrench of guilt. They'd been a part of him too long to disappear in a snap of the fingers. "At least not until a legal investigator arrived at my door with a form that would terminate my rights to her. Didn't you know, princess, that if my name was on the birth certificate she couldn't be adopted without my permission?"

Victoria turned away, answering mechanically, struggling against the horror of it all. "If it was explained, I didn't understand. There was a lot I didn't understand."

"Why did you agree to the adoption?"

"I thought I had no choice. Mother and Carlos insisted on abortion, so I bargained with all I had. Yes," she said almost angrily. "I agreed to go away. I agreed to the adoption. I would've agreed to anything to save my baby. I signed the papers. I meant to give her away, until I held her in my arms." Her lips tilted into a smile. The memory of the tiny black-haired child who had suckled at her breast was as vivid as yesterday. "Then I knew I couldn't."

"Were you ever really in Europe?"

"No." She said the name of an exclusive maternity home in upstate that Ben recognized. "I was to stay there until after the baby, then we were to resume with the plans as if I'd just recovered from an unfortunate accident."

"You mean Carlos still wanted the marriage?"

"He didn't care, Ben. It didn't matter that I'd had another man's child, so long as he wasn't saddled with it." She pulled her hand from under his and locked her fingers into tight fists. "And then I committed the unpardonable sin. I refused to give her up."

"That's when you were told that Lainie had died, and you walked away from the hospital." Ben didn't express his suspicion that the Mallorys and Carlos were behind the lie. It was unnecessary, for he saw in Victoria the ravages of a terrible hurt, the turning away from the dreadful thought.

"I didn't walk; I ran. For years I ran."

"And now you're home."

"No, you were right. This isn't home. It never was."

"It could be."

"What are you saying?" She was tensely guarded.

"I'm asking you to stay."

"But you hate me for Lainie, for almost losing her."

"I'm not so sure anymore." Ben met her look steadily. "Perhaps I did. I tried, but if I succeeded it's in the past."

"What about Lainie? What have you told her about me? What would you tell her now?" Once more only her eyes were alive, frightened, dreading, hopeful.

"All Lainie knows is that her mother's not with us. What we tell her in the future depends on the future itself."

"Won't she think it's peculiar that a strange woman arrived one day and never left?"

"She's accustomed to that sort of thing. Precious is forever collecting strays, both animal and human."

"I'd forgotten about Precious," Victoria said.

"She's known from the first who you were. If she hadn't, your delirium would've ended any doubts."

"And what about you? I saw your contempt. It can't be put aside so easily when you've spent years avenging yourself, collecting the pitiful remnants of what's left of the Mallory empire." She studied him very carefully as she asked shrewdly, "Is that what that lovely interlude in the bath was all about? Is that why you were so pleasant and caring and tender, calling me beautiful when we both know I'm not? Was it a performance? Were you winning me over? Am I to be a part of your collection, Ben? Will that make your revenge complete?"

Ben stood and walked to the balustrade that faced the castle. He lifted his face to the horizon and to the structure silhouetted against it. With a low sigh he turned back to Victoria. "It was never revenge, Victoria," he said. "If it had been, I would've dismantled the castle and the guesthouse stone by stone and wiped them from the face of Riverton. But I didn't, for someday, when the time is right, I plan to live there. You called it revenge, but you were wrong."

"Then why have you done this? Why would you want it?"

"For Lainie. I intend for her to have a background of wealth and power and social position. Then no one will ever dare judge her unsuitable for anything, or," he added quietly, "for anyone."

"Is that what happened to you, Ben?" She looked at him, wondering what deeply buried hurts he harbored.

"You might say that. But not anymore. I've discovered that money can open almost any door."

"I see. You'll open doors for Lainie that were closed for you, and in the meantime you'll give her everything you think will make her happy. Even a mother." There was a sadness deep inside Victoria as she

thought of another child who'd been given everything. The child who'd knocked at the door marked
love and, with all her wealth and privilege, couldn't
open it. She shivered in fear that Lainie might someday walk in her footsteps. Somehow she must make
Ben understand the danger in his ambition. "Castles
and social position don't promise happiness, nor do
pretty clothes or perfect grades.

"Nor could the mother you want so badly to give
her. Dear God! As much as I want to, I can't just step
back into her life. She wouldn't understand. It would
do her more harm than good."

"I know that," Ben admitted. "We won't rush
things. There are counselors and psychologists who
can advise us. Together we'll see that no harm comes
to her."

"It's not that simple." She traced the rim of the cup
with her fingers, hardly aware of what she did, wishing desperately that she could stay, that she could be
a part of Lainie's life.

"No, but it's a beginning." He walked back to the
table and stood looking down at her. "I know there
are no guarantees in this, but have there ever been in
life? We can only do the best we can. I have. I know
that you did. Victoria, look at me."

He waited until she moved her hands from the cup
and folded them in her lap. It seemed an eternity before she raised her face to his. "I asked you to stay. It
was the wrong question. Now that you've seen Lainie
needs you in ways that even I don't understand, my
question is, can you leave her?"

The hint of color that had gradually returned to her
cheeks receded. Her skin had grown translucent, as
fragile as delicate glass. Even the ragged moan that
accompanied the weary, agonized inclination of her

head seemed more than enough to shatter her. Still he waited. At last he heard the loneliness of a lifetime in her whispered answer.

"No, I could never leave her."

Five

___

Ben knew that silver eyes watched him; lost in thought, he felt the probing gaze. But he'd learned long ago that he wouldn't be hurried. Friend as well as physician, Dr. James Holland would lean back from his desk, fold his hands and wait.

"Her fever broke this afternoon," Ben said without turning from the shelves of books he'd prowled absently while waiting for Jim to finish with his last patient.

"I thought it might." There was pleasure in Jim's voice, not surprise. "How is she now?"

"Weak, tired, a bit confused. When I left them, Precious was hovering like a mother hen and Lainie was perched on Victoria's bed reading Dr. Seuss."

"Lainie's reading now, is she?"

"About the way you'd expect a prospective second grader to read. But she's been so anxious about Victoria, and wanted so desperately to help, that no one was going to tell her *Cat in the Hat* isn't exactly what an invalid needs. When I left, the two of them were having a wonderful time. You should see Victoria's face when she looks at Lainie." Ben massaged the taut muscles of his neck, and when he turned, his face was drawn and haggard. He had the look of a man who had, indeed, dwelt in Purgatory. "My God! What she's been through."

"She's told you?"

"Not intentionally."

"Delirium." Jim spread his long fingers on the desk before him. He, too, had suffered through bits of Victoria's tortured monologue. "Malaria isn't pretty. Have you any idea where she contracted it?"

Ben's features twisted in a waking nightmare. He still heard her mutterings of fire and danger. But, he reminded himself, it hadn't been all bad. There had been laughter and love and a sense of self-worth in her feverish revelations. He knew he mustn't dwell on the dark side; Victoria hadn't.

"Where, Ben?" Jim prompted.

"Somewhere in South America near a small banana plantation there's a village very aptly called Purgatory. She spent the past seven years there."

"How was it our Vicky came to be there?"

"I have no idea how she came to be in such an isolated place. I only know she worked in a small clinic there."

"Then why the hell didn't she have preventive medication!" Jim's mild tone rose to an unusual volume as he paused in the act of reaching for his pipe.

"Most of the medical supplies were destroyed. Apparently from the little that was saved she kept none for herself. She meant to get medication here if she needed it."

"A bit after the fact," Jim said wryly.

Ben stopped pacing and faced Jim grimly. "She tried to tell me by the lake that she needed it. I wouldn't listen."

"Don't blame yourself, Ben. It was too late already." Jim switched subjects adroitly. "Is that how she burned her hands? Trying to save the supplies?"

"I don't know."

"It's the sort of thing she'd do, with no thought for her own safety," Jim observed over an unlighted pipe.

"There're gaps in her past. I don't know what happened in Purgatory—how she got there, why she left or where she was going. I don't know where she got her medical training.

"None of that matters. The important thing is she's home." For the first time since he had entered the office, Ben took a chair, but the strained lines of his body did not relax. In a revealing gesture of deepseated worry, he pressed thumb and fingers against the bridge of his nose. His eyes, when he lifted them, were turbulent. He'd paid a double toll, fighting Victoria's illness and his own emotions, as well.

"What do I do, Jim?" There was a ragged touch of desperation in the low appeal.

"About Lainie and Vicky?" In all the years that Ben had known Jim, it was his first admission that he'd guessed the truth. It had hovered between them, unspoken, understood.

Ben knew that Jim had treated Victoria from birth. In those distant days of friendship she'd told him how this compassionate man had cared for her through the hurts and illnesses of childhood. She would turn to him first in a time of trouble. He'd likely been first to know of her pregnancy.

Jim was astute. Ben had little doubt that one look at Lainie and he'd known. Yet his questions went unasked, his suspicions unconfirmed. Instead he'd served as tireless mentor for an unprepared father.

"Is it ironic or prophetic that on the very day Victoria arrived, Lainie announced she wanted a mother?" Bewildered blue eyes found comfort in silver.

"What do *you* want, Ben?" Jim looked kindly at the man who'd put his own life aside for the love of a child.

Ben's gaze strayed to the window, seeking the silent strength of cloud-shrouded mountains. Yet when he looked back at Jim, their serenity had escaped him. "I want them both. I want to keep them with me and protect them. But can I?" He was filled with a fearful uncertainty. "They're both so fragile. One mistake and both could be hurt."

"I think you underestimate them," Jim suggested. "Lainie's a happy, well-adjusted child, and Vicky's grown into a strong woman. She's a survivor."

"Can we ever tell Lainie the truth?"

"Do you want to?"

"Yes, of course I do, but it's not that simple. The one thing Victoria could not survive would be for Lainie to hate her. And at the same time, wouldn't it destroy Victoria to live so closely to her own child and not tell her?"

"No one will be destroyed, Ben. Not Lainie, not Victoria, not you," Jim said with a confidence that was contagious. "All you need to do is go slowly. I took the liberty of consulting a colleague. He agrees that you should give Lainie time. Let her assume Victoria's simply another of Precious's waifs. Let them spend a few weeks together. Or, if that's what's needed, months. They must know each other.

"When the time's right, tell her, but only what she can comprehend. You'll know when that time comes; you'll recognize it as naturally as you breathe. When she's older, tell her the whole story. She's a loving, sweet-natured child. She'll understand."

"There'll be questions. Lainie looks more and more like Victoria. Someone's bound to notice. Precious did."

"I think the problem will be solved long before you should worry. As to passing the word and supplying explanations in the village about Victoria's return...why don't you leave that to Precious and me."

A spark of hope found sustenance as Ben put desperate faith in Jim's wisdom. "What will you say?"

"Just enough of the truth to make it believable. That Victoria was ill for a long while. That she spent years out of the country and hadn't been able to return."

"Will it be enough to satisfy the curiosity?"

"It will if I say so," Jim grumbled, and the younger man didn't doubt the veracity of his statement.

"As you did when I brought Lainie home," Ben said in dawning comprehension. "What half-truths did you tell then?"

"The obvious." Jim was unabashed. "That Lainie was your child but that for reasons of her own the mother couldn't be with you."

"Then you glowered and dared them not to believe."

"Something like that."

"No one's ever seen you truly angry, Jim. Considering your size, I think it would be something to behold. Perhaps that's part of the mystique and why they respect your warning.''

"I've got a warning for you."

Ben searched his face for signs of his ponderous levity and found none. Jim was deadly serious. A twinge of unease flickered in Ben. "About Victoria?''

"She's a mature woman now, and she's had to be very strong. Don't let that strength fool you. She's very vulnerable. Be careful with her. Don't make any—''

"Dammit! Jim," Ben said hotly as the big man touched a nerve. "Are you warning me to keep my hands off her? Do you think I'd force myself on her?''

"No, Ben. I don't.'' Jim continued, unperturbed. "I'm trying to point out that the attraction between you is explosive. It always was. Lainie's living proof. Is it any different now? I'm advising caution, nothing more. Don't get so caught up in your concern over Lainie that you forget about yourselves. Whatever happens between you, be sure it's the right thing, for the right reasons. For both of you.''

"She's been hurt enough.'' Ben's temper subsided as quickly as it had flared. "I wouldn't add more.''

"I never thought you would, not intentionally.''

"Sorry.'' Ben shrugged an apology. "I'm on edge. I didn't mean to jump down your throat.''

"I know. You're going to be walking a tightrope for some little time. But I can take one worry off your mind. I'm pretty certain Vicky will be fine, but why don't you bring her in and let me discuss the next stage of treatment needed to resolve the problem for good?''

"I'll do that.'' Ben stood, half turned toward the door. "We'll be expecting you to stop by for dinner some night soon. You're always welcome. Precious and Lainie look forward to your visits, and I'm sure Victoria would enjoy it."

"I'll be there. And Ben." Jim waited until Ben faced him. "Clayton and Elizabeth were just too old and too self-centered to have a daughter like Vicky. They weren't evil."

"Weren't they?" Ben's voice was frosty. "Would you say that if I told you that it was after Victoria retracted the adoption that she was told Lainie had died? Can you think of any reason for it? Who cared except the Mallorys?"

"You can't be sure they were responsible."

"No, I can't. I have a lot of questions that have no answers, but none are as important as that one. It's the one answer I intend to have. For Victoria's sake. As soon as I'm sure she's recovering, I'll have it for her."

Jim nodded his agreement; argument would be useless, in any case. "She'll be a while recovering mentally and emotionally, but barring complications, she should be physically fit within a couple of weeks."

"I'll leave for the maternity hospital in two weeks, then," Ben said tersely. "You'll watch over her?"

"Of course."

"Thank you." Ben grinned ruefully; his request had been insultingly ridiculous. With a return to graciousness, he nodded a brief goodbye and left the room, leaving Jim to muse over his pipe long after the door had closed behind him.

Victoria lay half sleeping, half dreaming, basking by the pool as she had almost every day for the past three weeks. The sun warmed her, seeping into her, casting over her a glow that matched the light in her eyes. She grew stronger and happier each day. Life was perfect. Perfect as long as she didn't let herself think of her parents and the lie that had cost her precious years of her daughter's life. Perfect as long as she didn't think of Ben and his need to build an empire and possess a castle. Perfect as long as she didn't dwell on the unexpected and mysterious business trip that had swept him from her life almost a week ago. Perfect, for Lainie liked her. Someday soon Lainie might even come to love her. Then she could lie in the sun as she did now, savoring it, and nothing else would matter.

There was no sound, no warning, only a prickling sensation across her skin. A sudden rush of coolness flowed over her as a shadow blocked the sun. She opened her eyes and found herself staring into Ben's worried face.

"Ben! You're back!"

"Are you all right?" Anxiety tumbled from him. After her recovery, fear for her had become his unwelcome but inescapable companion. "You were so still!"

"Of course I'm all right."

"Are you sure?"

"I was a little tired. Lainie and I took a walk down to the lake. On the way back it became crashingly clear I'd overestimated my strength. Precious ordered me to rest by the pool. I guess I'm not as young as I used to be," she joked.

"But every bit as foolhardy. Out of bed only a few weeks and you decide to take a little stroll. To the lake and back must be more than a mile." The scowl that had lightened under her reassurance returned in force.

"Good heavens! On the plantation, a mile was nothing," she protested. "I walked farther than that many times to deliver a baby. Then hours later, often without having slept, I walked back."

"On the plantation, my sweet little witch doctor, you hadn't just recovered from malaria, and I doubt you were so fragile that the slightest breeze would sail away with you." He called her the teasing title the natives had given her as she practiced midwifery among them. He'd laughed with her when she'd told him of the name and guessed at the shy respect in it. He'd laughed and teased her then, but his unsettling surge of concern had wiped away any shred of humor.

His probing inspection wandered over every curve as he sought out every ounce of added flesh with unwavering thoroughness. Memories and the promise of her thin body had merged into reality. Under Precious's loving care and in the company of her child, Victoria flourished. She'd been mistaken when she'd thought she couldn't step abruptly into Lainie's life. She was exactly what Lainie needed, and the child worshiped her. She'd become mother in all but name, and it filled her with an abiding joy that enchanted her. Victoria had become a ravishing woman who, in her tawny beauty, put the young princess to shame.

Ben drew a sudden rough breath, and a glittering light spun out of control in the blue of his eyes.

Riveted by the look of him, Victoria felt a faint excitement stir within her. For the first time she remembered that she lay in sleepy carelessness, clothed only in the tiniest of bikinis. A telltale stain of golden apricot crept over her cheeks. Her fingers skittered across the surface of the lounge to clutch at his shirt that she'd commandeered as a robe.

"Are you cold?" His voice barely rippled the stillness of the garden.

She thought of saying yes, of sweeping the silken fabric of his shirt about her in that pretense. But it was a lie, and he would know. A negative shake of her head set her hair astir about her shoulders.

"Then don't."

"Why?" Her gaze roved over him. Sunlight struck silver in his hair. His jacket hung from one crooked finger over his shoulder. The ice blue of his shirt matched his eyes exactly, its tapered lines clinging to the lines of his body. There was tension in that hard proud posture, as if whether or not she chose to shield her body from him carried some odd significance. Her questioning eyes searched his.

"Why?" she asked again in the softest of whispers.

"Because I like to look at you."

The blunt admission startled her. Her fingers jerked, tightening. The only sound was the lazy lapping of the pool as a breeze danced over it. He was immobile. Waiting. Watching. Slowly her fingers released the shirt, sending it slithering to the stone that edged the pool. And something delicious and intimate shimmered between them.

"I think I'll join you," he said. With a quick flick of his wrist he tossed his jacket carelessly into a nearby chair and, without looking away from her, began to slip his tie from its perfect knot and unbuttoned his shirt. One shrug and it lay in a forgotten heap at his feet.

"No, princess," he said when her lips parted in surprise as his hand rested at his belt, "Just the belt. No more. No striptease. Not this time."

His laugh was attractive and captivating. She caught the sudden lightness of his mood, welcomed it and matched it in kind. "Should I be disappointed?"

"Well, I'd never look quite as good as you do in that tiny green thing. But I have it from a great authority that I'm devastation in my new black trunks."

"Devastation?" She grinned and relaxed for the first time since he'd cast his shadow over her. Deliberately she looked at him again. At the smooth play of muscles that rippled beneath the bronzed skin. At the thatch of dark hair that covered his chest, then thinned into a tantalizing line that disappeared beyond his slacks. He *was* devastation. "I'd say—" she grinned mischievously "—that Lainie and Precious have exquisite taste."

His mouth drew down in a grimace, but a pleased expression crinkled his face. "How did you guess?"

"Who else has such an inventive vocabulary?"

"Who else, indeed." He stretched out on a lounge beside her, catching her hand in his.

The sun bore down from a cloudless sky. Somewhere, deep in its leafy hideaway, a mockingbird sang its heart out. A breeze teased the treetops, then swooped and swirled about them to touch their bodies with kiss of coolness.

"Hmm," he sighed. "Nice."

"Very." Victoria smiled and was glad that after days of loneliness, Ben was home.

"Miss me?"

"Terribly."

"Good."

"How was your trip?" At her idle question the rhythmic stroke of his thumb across her hand stopped. The mockingbird grew quiet; the breeze dwindled. Even the blazing light of the sun seemed to darken. A tension had entered the garden.

"It was . . . productive." Ben's hand gripped hers as he swung his feet to the side and sat up. His gaze was on her, lingering at her mouth. "I've spent the past two days at the hospital where Lainie was born."

"What!" Victoria sat up abruptly. She was filled with an escalating dread. "Why?"

"Because the answer to the question that's eating you alive was there."

"I don't know what you mean," she lied, evading his searching look, afraid of what she might read there.

"Victoria." He reached for her other hand, catching it in his. "Your parents weren't responsible for what happened."

"They weren't?" She seemed not to understand, then there was a sudden blaze of happy light striking gold in her brown eyes. "They truly weren't?"

"No. It was a crazy misunderstanding. There was a very young student nurse who was new to the hospital. Do you remember?"

Victoria shook her head. "There were so many new faces."

"It's not necessary that you remember, only that you understand it was her first taste of tragedy."

"Tragedy?"

"A baby did die, Victoria," he said gently.

"No!" Even in the happiness of finding her own child, Victoria grieved for a lost, nameless baby.

"A newborn she'd been caring for in the nursery. When she came to your room she was in shock from it, and then you spoke of your own baby. She broke down. All she could think was that a tiny girl had died. Perhaps it was even more traumatic because the baby was perfectly healthy until she just stopped breathing. What you heard was the hysteria of a child-woman facing her first taste of death.

"It wasn't until hours later, long after she'd regained control, that she realized you might've misunderstood. By then it was too late. You were gone. They searched for you, of course, but there was never a trace.''

"I don't remember where I went myself," she said. "My first recollection was days later. I don't know where I'd been or what I'd done, but I found myself miles away in a different city, sitting in a small church, thinking my world had come to an end."

"But it hadn't."

"No, it hadn't." She clasped his hands tighter. "I found friends who helped me survive, and Lainie came to you."

"Why, Victoria?" It was a stark question of grave significance.

"You're asking why I put your name on the birth certificate."

"You didn't have to, you know. I doubt most girls do. Why did you?" He waited, his eyes capturing hers, holding them as if his world depended on her answer.

She met his look steadily. "I couldn't stand for our baby not to have some part of you. Instead of a blank line, I could give one small gift to her. She could have her true father, even if it was only for a few days."

Ben felt the tight twisting ache of need and hope uncoil inside him. Victoria had given him a gift, as well. Only a single glittering drop that shimmered briefly on his thick dark lashes and the relaxing of his tense shoulders betrayed the effect of her words. Understanding that remembering was as painful for her as it was for him, he asked, "Have you never wondered why I kept the name you'd given her?"

"I wondered," Victoria answered honestly. "I was afraid to ask."

"At first I was in such a state of shock I wasn't thinking of names."

"It must've been terrible," she said.

"You couldn't imagine. A pompous little ass named Phinias T. Crowe arrived at my door with this tacky little legal form, telling me very calmly that I had a daughter and assuming beyond a shadow of a doubt that I'd be glad to terminate my rights to her. I thought he'd made a mistake or lost his mind. Then he said your name and I was certain I'd lost mine."

"Weren't you ever tempted to sign the paper and forget you'd ever heard the name Mallory?"

"I can't deny that I thought of it. Every possibility crossed my mind. But there it was before me, the birth records with three names. Yours, Lainie's and mine. In the end I knew what I wanted to do. I would bring my daughter home. I would create a life and a heritage for her. She would be the woman her mother should have been, and no one would ever question who she was. The one thing I couldn't give her was her mother, but like you, I could give her something. The name her mother had chosen."

Victoria could perceive the shock and confusion he must have felt. She wondered at the honor of such a man, to rearrange his own life and his ambitions for the sake of a child thrust upon him. No, not thrust—accepted, willingly and lovingly. Her gratitude for that willingness made it easier to hide the disappointment that the name Lainie was no more than a part of a so-called heritage. She had blindly hoped it had in some way been a measure of love.

But Ben had never been her lover in the truest sense of the word. He had been her friend. She smiled at him. "So you brought her home, found Precious for her and loved her."

"Loving Lainie is an easy thing to do."

"Thank you, Ben." Beyond the happiness on her face hovered a tinge of sadness, and Ben remembered a child who had never been loved.

He freed one hand from hers to stroke the shining fall of hair from her forehead. Then he cupped her chin in his palm, lifting her averted gaze to his. His thumb brushed lightly over her cheek, catching the spill of a tear.

"Princess, in their own way Clayton and Elizabeth loved you. They just didn't know how to show it. They made a lot of mistakes because they were unable to bend. I'm sure that in their own narrow-minded way they thought they were doing the right things for you. Even when they arranged a marriage with a bastard like Carlos. And in the end...they lost something very dear." Ben faltered in his effort to ease the hurts of the past. Then, with regained composure, he continued. "Jim told me they weren't evil, but I had to find out for myself, and for you. That's why I had to go to the hospital."

"I think that next to finding Lainie, the most wonderful thing that's happened in my life in a long time is that you cared enough to find the truth for me. I'll always be grateful for that, Ben. I've spent a lifetime learning forgiveness. But that would've been too much. I couldn't have forgiven them if they'd taken her from me with a lie."

"There was no lie, princess, only a terrible mistake," Ben said. "Can you rest easy now that you know?"

"Yes, I can. At least about the past. It's the future that frightens me."

"There's no reason. We're going to take one day at a time and make the best of it. Life's a gamble. Nobody has any guarantees. Why should we be any different?'' He untangled his other hand from hers to cup her face with both. "I'm going to kiss you just once. Because I've missed you, old friend. Then I'm going to lie with you in the sun."

His dark head bent to hers, shielding her from a world of hurt and trouble. It was a gentle kiss that touched flame to tinder, the heat of it warming more than her lips, whetting an unslaked yearning.

Ben's mouth held hers, soft and undemanding. Happiness caught at her in a spangled radiance as an aching tenderness for this big, tough, gentle man set her atremble. A sweet, flowing hunger swept through her, and he became the sun in her world. Her arms went about him, holding him close, crushing his hair-roughened chest to her barely clad breasts. Rejoicing in the feel of him against her skin, she returned his kiss, and in an instant of wild delight, her tongue touched his, caressing, savoring; retreating, returning; drawing from him a low, ragged groan.

The shock of her own boldness and the sound of his cry brought her shatteringly back to reality. Her hands slid to his chest, her palm resting over the thunder of his heart. He was enchantment, exciting and frightening. When she would have drawn away, his fingers wound into her hair, creating a kaleidoscope of sensations that left no room for fear. She melted back into him with a whispered sigh.

Ben lifted his head reluctantly. His eyes were warm and glittering like the summer sky as they held hers. A lazy finger traced lightly as a whisper over the swell of her lips.

"Thank you for that, princess," he murmured.

"I . . ."

"Shh." He laid a finger across her lips. "Don't say anything. Not just yet. For now, just let me hold you."

She made no objection when he leaned her back against the pillow of the chaise lounge, or when he fitted his body to hers. Her hips nestled into the curve of his. Lean, tautly muscled legs clad in elegant slacks tangled with the bare, shapely length of hers. The beat of his heart was strong at her back. His arm was flung over her, his hand resting between her breasts. The tips of long, slender fingers burrowed beneath the scrap of emerald to lie against the bud of a nipple, their very stillness a caress. His breathing quieted as if in touching her he found peace.

As she drifted into sleep with him, there was neither hate nor forgiveness. There was only contentment, the sun and the sky and Ben.

Six

A spate of giggles accompanied the sound of running feet. The kitchen door was flung open in a rush, and Lainie dashed through it. The tail of a shirt that had once been Victoria's flapped comically about her knees.

"I won! I won!" Lainie clapped her hands and grinned cheekily at Victoria, who leaned against the frame of the door, gasping for breath.

"I can see that I need practice if I'm going to race you." Victoria tousled the tumbled black curls and leaned to drop a kiss on a flushed, chubby cheek.

Neither was aware that Precious stopped as she was emerging from the pantry, struck by their strong similarity. A similarity that had become more apparent each day of the past five weeks. As the look of wholesome good health had put a youthful brightness into Victoria's complexion and a golden flush to her cheeks, it had become easy to imagine that their faces were past and future.

But for the mass of heavy black hair, Lainie looked amazingly like a young Victoria. It required no great feat of deduction to recognize in the child the beginnings of the elegance and beauty that had come to the mature woman.

When they were clad almost identically in bikinis and loose shirts, it would be obvious to any but the most unobservant that they were mother and daughter. The resemblance extended beyond the physical. Their mannerisms, the stubborn tilt of a chin, the grave expression when concerned, the crinkle of a smile, were disconcertingly the same.

"Glory be!" Precious declared. "Like two peas in a pod. They'd best be getting something settled soon. Before someone notices and talks out of turn."

"Precious!" Victoria exclaimed. "I didn't see you."

"I was just trying to decide which of you was the youngest," the housekeeper groused, her elbows bent at her sides in unconvincing irritation. "How's a body supposed to get any work done around here? It's near to impossible! 'Specially with the two of you about. Upsetting my kitchen, running in and out like a pack of wild Indians. And both of you nearly as brown. All either of you lacks is a feather."

"Sorry." Victoria flashed her an unrepentant grin. "Lainie challenged me to a foot race, the loser forfeits her drumstick at dinner tonight."

"And how is it you're so sure we'll be having fried chicken tonight, Miss Smarts?" Precious asked. "Have you been playing at detective?"

"Just call me Sherlock Smarts." Victoria struggled to assume a serious expression as she held up three fingers. "Number one, my dear Watson. You went shopping this morning. You always do that when Jim's coming to dinner. Number two, fried chicken is his favorite.''

"And Daddy's, too," Lainie added. "When he called last night he said he'd be home today."

"But maybe not in time for dinner, darling," Victoria reminded her. "He doubted he'd be finished with his business until too late for any but the midnight flight."

"Can we leave him some for a midnight snack?"

"I don't see why not. In fact, I'll bet Precious had already planned to."

"Of course, child." Precious smiled down at Lainie. "I haven't let your daddy starve yet, have I?"

"No, not ever," Lainie said seriously. She turned back to Victoria, ready to resume their game. "I forgot. How else did we know about the chicken?"

"Clue number three," Victoria continued. "And our most conclusive. The heavenly odor that's been wafting over the garden for the past half hour."

"We got hungry and hungrier," the youngest chimed in.

"Mad with hunger." Victoria grinned down at Lainie.

"Worse and worser." Giggling, Lainie followed her cue.

Victoria stepped to the stove in a dancing half turn and lifted the lid from a large skillet. "Mmm. What did I tell you? Proof positive, and delicious! Surely you can forgive a couple of mad Indians when it's your fault we're mad."

"Ha!" Precious tapped the back of Victoria's hand with a wooden spoon. "Put that lid back on before you burn yourself, and don't try any more of your flattery on me, young lady. Just remember you're not too old or too big for me to take you over my knee." Hollows formed beneath her full cheeks as she bit down on them in a futile effort to suppress a grin.

"Precious—" Lainie giggled through fingers that covered her mouth "—you say that, but you never do it."

"There's always a first time." Precious tried to glare, failed miserably and succumbed to laughter. "Here—" she placed a bowl of peaches in the center of the table "—have one of these to tide you over until dinner, then scat."

"How beautiful! They're nearly perfect." Victoria took one for herself and handed another to Lainie. "Did the young couple from the farm bring them? I thought I caught a glimpse of them as I took a walk through the garden. I'd like to meet them someday, but they always seem to avoid me."

"They're a mite shy."

"And generous."

"To a fault," Precious agreed. "They brought these this morning on their way to the market. They grow the best peaches in the country."

"They must require a lot of work and special care." Victoria grinned at Lainie and handed her a napkin to wipe away the juice that trickled down her chin.

"Work, care and prayer that God will keep a halter on Mother Nature and her late-spring frosts."

"And one of the prayers is yours." Victoria had no doubts.

"Well," Precious admitted, "I'm not above getting down on my knees to help a friend."

"Precious." Victoria stood on tiptoe to kiss a waffled cheek. "I love you. Every day I discover how nice it is to have a friend like you."

Victoria was enveloped in a hug that threatened her ribs. "And you make every day a pleasure. You've brought sunshine into all our lives."

"Now," Precious added gruffly as she released her. "Go on with you and get dressed for dinner. Wear that pretty new frock I got you in town the other day. The one that shows off your bosom."

"For shame!" Victoria clapped her free hand over one of Lainie's ears in mock horror. In her light-hearted mood she didn't think to wonder, in case of what? "Precious, you wicked woman. Whatever will poor Lainie think of such talk?"

"What's a bosom?" the child asked around a mouthful of fruit, addressing the question to Victoria.

"It's...uh..." Victoria fumbled, not sure how much or how little she should explain. "When a girl becomes a woman she grows..." She looked desperately to Precious for help.

"Pillows." With a word Precious resolved her dilemma.

"Oh!" Lainie brightened as she looked from Precious's pendulous breasts to Victoria's smaller, shaplier ones. "Your bosom's pretty, Victoria," she chirped happily. "I like the way it jiggles when you laugh."

"Jiggle!" Victoria protested with a laugh. "I do *not* jiggle." She laughed again and couldn't keep herself from looking down curiously at the part in question. She never knew which came first: Lainie's triumphant "See, I told you," Precious's booming guffaw, or her own wild, scarlet blush.

"Oh, dear. I'd better quit while I'm ahead," she said decisively. Drawing about herself a fleeting composure that threatened to crumble into undignified giggles, she prattled in theatrical hauteur, "I shall retreat to my room. You may call me when dinner is served."

Victoria whirled in a dramatic pirouette. Her pretended arrogance lasted all of the split second it took to realize that Ben stood in the doorway. Weary, haggard, with deep lines about his mouth, yet unbelievably vital.

With something like a grimace, his appraisal touched every inch of bare flesh and lingered on the coral strip across her breasts. His stare was relentless, the weight of it marking her like a brand.

A responsive shock arced through her with an incandescence of blue fire, its blazing heat usurping her strength, paralyzing all but the violent lurch of her heart. One part of her tingled with the need to reach for the gaping edges of the shirt she wore to pull it tighter about her. Another insane part wanted to discard it and step into his arms and feel the brush of his body against her own.

Victoria realized in that instant how long the week had been. How much she'd missed him and ached for the sight of him. "Ben," she whispered as her hands hung by her side in indecision. "We didn't expect you back so soon."

"So I see," he said, and looked in open admiration at the nearly nonexistent bikini she'd never dared wear when he was home.

"Daddy!" Lainie skipped by Victoria and launched herself at him.

"How's my girl?" Ben scooped the child into his arms, but his gaze hadn't left Victoria.

"Fine." Lainie threw her arms about his neck.

"What've you been up to while I've been gone?" he asked as he nuzzled the hollow at her ear.

"Mostly we've been at the pool getting brown as Indians."

"Or as berries." Ben added his own cliché as he touched the collar of the shirt that swallowed the child. "What's this?"

"It's what we wear to cover up our suits when we leave the pool," Lainie explained, implying great patience with his ignorance. "Girls do that."

"Oh, they do, do they?"

"Um-hmm. It's for mod..." The child struggled with an unfamiliar word.

"For modesty's sake?" he supplied. He lifted his head, turning a speculative look from Victoria to Precious and back again to Victoria, wondering who felt the need for modesty.

"That's what Victoria said when she gave me this. She said I needed a big shirt to cover my bikini."

"It's big enough," he said with a laugh.

"Yep. Victoria's is almost as big."

"It's a bit roomy," he agreed as his eyes traveled over her again in a flicker of recognition. The shirt Victoria wore was his. The one he'd dressed her in the day her fever had broken. The same one she hadn't worn the day he'd returned from the maternity hospital and found her by the pool. It had apparently become a standard part of her wardrobe. Ben wondered why.

"I hope you don't mind." Victoria grew flustered, guessing his thoughts. She pulled nervously at a button. "It's comfortable, and Precious said you rarely wore it."

"You're a definite improvement. It never looked so good on me."

Lainie reclaimed his attention. "We didn't expect you yet, and we didn't hear you come in, Daddy."

"Considering the chatter I heard, it's no wonder," he teased her.

"We were discussing Victoria's bosom. We think it's pretty."

"Lainie." Victoria groaned under her breath.

"Do you think it's pretty, Daddy?" the little girl asked in all earnestness.

"Lainie!" Victoria's moan became a wail of distress.

She pointedly ignored the low-pitched chuckle that came from the stove where Precious pretended innocence as she worked diligently over the frying chicken.

"I think it's time you had a bath, young lady." Ben bent to set the child on the floor. "Run on up to your room. I'll be there in a second to help you with your hair. How would you like to wear your new dress to dinner, since Dr. Jim's coming?"

"The very newest one with the pretty sash?" Lainie had been very skillfully diverted, much to Victoria's relief.

"The very same," Ben assured the child. "But not until you've had a bath, so you'd better hurry."

With a playful swat on her bottom from her father, Lainie scurried away. When Ben straightened, Victoria realized her reprieve was to be short-lived. Wickedness danced in his eyes, and a look of mischief wreathed his face. He looked years younger, and if not handsome, then damnably attractive. She felt the sudden urge to run, and it must have been apparent. Ben's arm draped firmly over her shoulder, drawing her to him, effectively hampering her flight.

His jacket was open, and before she ducked her head to avoid his laughing eyes, she had a moment to realize how well the mauve of his shirt suited his dark skin. There was nothing feminine about the delicate color, and only a fool would have disagreed.

"You can come up for air now, Precious." He tossed the remark over his shoulder as he turned Victoria toward the hall. "I'm going to walk Victoria to her room."

"Dinner's at seven." The suspiciously bland remark was accompanied by a rattle of pot lids.

"We'll see you then." Before Victoria could add anything or protest, he guided her from the room.

"I do know the way to my own room," she said in a low voice, not trusting herself to say more.

"Of course you do. But since mine is next door, why shouldn't I have the pleasure of your company for the stroll up the stairs?"

"Because..." She cast about for an excuse to escape from the exciting grip of his hand on her shoulder. As it had quite often of late, her traitorous mind refused to cooperate.

Ben stopped short and waited until she lifted her questioning face to his. "Because?"

She dropped her gaze, unable to hold and challenge his. The truth suddenly occurred to her. She was not being given a choice. Her "because" might satisfy his curiosity or even give him greater cause for amusement, but it would make no difference. She shrugged beneath the confident pressure of his arm and, as graciously as she could manage, accepted her defeat.

"No reason, I guess." She sighed. "None at all."

"Good girl." Ben laughed. "It's the wise warrior who knows when to retreat."

Victoria had no answer for his remark. She was fresh out of quick, dazzling repartee. Ben guided her across the hall, then climbed the stairs with her in companionable silence. The journey down the hall to her room was as quiet.

She had begun to think she'd been spared his mischief when he stopped with her outside her door. She'd stepped from beneath the shelter of his arm, her hand on the latch having almost made her escape complete, when his fingers curled over the collar of her shirt.

"To the victor," Ben murmured as he tugged gently, drawing her toward him. "At least for the moment."

There was an unnerving quality about his long, deep study of her, and the same sensations she'd felt when she'd first seen him standing darkly attractive in the kitchen exploded inside her. As he brought her hard against him, body and thigh, her head tilted back instinctively.

The light was behind him, its shining halo catching fire in the silver in his hair. There was a sudden urge in Victoria to put her hands in the wiry strands and draw his lips down to hers. In a betrayal of her thoughts, her eyes moved to the enticing line of his mouth. It had been three weeks since the afternoon in the garden when he'd held her and kissed her.

His hands slid under her shirt and closed about her waist, almost spanning it. His fingers splaying over her ribs were strong and tight and unthreatening, but something inside her fluttered like a frightened bird. She tensed and waited, but he did not transgress.

From some deep unthinking part of her a wild impatience rose like a fever, surging into a driving need. In unconscious invitation she moved, arching her body into his. When his mouth covered hers in response, she expected his lips to be demanding in a shared urgency. Instead his kiss was frustrating in its gentleness. Then, incredibly, he was moving away.

"Mmm. Delicious." He teased against her trembling mouth. "You should always wear peaches. They suit you."

"What?" Victoria looked blankly up at him, unable to comprehend anything except that she wanted his lips on hers.

Ben slipped his hands from her body. With exaggerated care he folded the shirt tighter about her. "It's nearly seven. You'd better hurry."

"I know," she said. Confused by his withdrawal, she scanned his face intently for some sign of strain or stress and found none. His features were as calm and solemn as if the interlude had never happened.

He leaned past her to open her door, then turned her away from him. Victoria thought he meant to release her, but she was mistaken. Stepping close behind her with his hands on her shoulders, he pulled her back against the wall of his chest. His breath fluttered warmly in the fall of her hair as he spoke in a husky whisper. "Lainie's right, you know. Your bosom is pretty. Wear something that shows it off. I can't touch, but there's no law that says I can't look." With an easy push he propelled her into her room, closing the door behind her.

Victoria leaned weakly against dark wooden panels, listening to his retreating footsteps. Her mind tumbled in chaos. She wasn't sure what had just happened. Ben was becoming more and more an enigma. One minute he was the caring and protective friend she'd always known. In the next he touched her with the smoldering, dangerous look of a lover. Then inexplicably, as he'd just done, he would draw away and tease her as he did Lainie. Or as he had the princess.

Princess. A name from the past, as unreal as the child she'd been. Why, after all that had happened, did Ben still call her princess? Did he look for the girl she'd been? Slowly Victoria pushed away from the door and crossed the room. She slipped into the chair before a dressing table. Looking into the eyes that stared back at her, she searched for the real Victoria. Time sped away from her as she reached into the depths of herself.

Despite the care Precious lavished on her, she was still thinner than she'd once been. Time had honed her body with the leanness of maturity, and tragedy had instilled a worldly wisdom in her eyes. The innocence that had led her once to seek a night of stolen love with no thought to consequences had long been destroyed. In her mirrored image, Victoria saw a woman who'd lived a lifetime in a span of a few years. One who'd loved briefly, paid dearly the price of rebellion, then built a new life on the ruins. Each passing day of pain and success had left its mark of change.

"I can't be that young girl again, Ben," she cried in an aching half sob. "Not even for you. It's too late."

The strains of Ben's whistle as he returned from Lainie's room to the adjoining room jolted her from her thoughts. One quick glance at the clock on the bedside table warned her she had little time. It was only as she was rising to bathe and dress that she realized she held the half-eaten peach in her hand.

After a hurried bath, Victoria stood before an open closet, studying its contents with a critical eye. The dresses that crowded the rack had been chosen by Precious, whose disdain for conservative clothing was often quite evident. Now Victoria found that the housekeeper's flamboyant creed, "If you've got it, flaunt it," suited her own purpose nicely.

One hand clutched the huge towel to her breasts while the other riffled impatiently through the colorful array of expensive clothing. Occasionally she would hesitate, consider, then shake her head and move on to the next garment. Then she found it. A wisp of pale tawny nothing that would be demonstrable proof that she was a woman. Ben would meet the real Victoria.

Bless you, Precious. Victoria mentally thanked the woman for her foresighted insistence that she not return this particular gown, which so closely resembled the one she'd worn in the portrait that had once hung over the mantel downstairs. While the dress was similar, she knew the fit would be quite different. It would be perfect.

A tap rattled her door. "Ready, princess?"

"Just a minute." She looked down at her nakedness, draped carelessly by velour. A delighted grin crossed her lips. "Why not?" she wondered aloud thoughtfully to herself. "I can't begin any sooner."

On bare feet she half danced her way to the door. After one daring adjustment of her towel, she opened the door a sliver, allowing just enough view of her bare skin to intrigue.

Ben had discarded coat and tie and dressed in comfortable summer casuals. Impossibly rested, and rakishly handsome in their close fit, he was leaning against the wall in loose-limbed languor that deserted him at the first glimpse of her faintly damp womanliness nearly spilling from its covering.

"What the hell." He came abruptly away from the wall with a look of astonishment blazing like fury in his shocked face.

"I didn't mean to take so long." She rushed in before he could finish his growled outburst. Opening the door a fraction more and dropping the towel to the last point of virtue, she gave him her best and most guileless smile. "I don't know what happened, Ben. I guess I just lost track of the time."

From the corridor there was only a low, inarticulate sound suspiciously like a groan.

"I was wondering." She lifted her leg from the folds of the towel with a sly innocence. With her toes pointed elegantly, she extended and arched it for his inspection, exposing the curve of her hip from thigh to waist. "Should I wear stockings, or do you think my tan—"

"Dammit, Victoria!" he interrupted her roughly. "I don't care what you wear. Just wear *something*."

Blithely exultant in her triumph, she shifted the towel imperceptibly. Her arms crossed tightly, discreetly, at her breasts, casting the intriguing cleft between them into deep shadowy contour. In pretense she was magnificently unaware and naive as she looked up at him. "I don't have a bra that's suitable. Do you think—"

"Heaven help me!" The rumbling cry was torn from him in a fierce plea.

"Did I say something wrong?" She blinked in dismayed surprise at his outburst.

"Get dressed, Victoria. Now." His voice was grim, and even as he spun violently away she felt the impact of his look. "I'll wait for you downstairs in the foyer."

He'd disappeared beyond the landing before she shut the door. Her triumph was sweet. He hadn't called her princess. Not once! Score one for Victoria.

"And I'm not through with you yet," she promised the absent man as she tossed the towel aside and considered the clinging fabric of the dress she'd chosen.

Undergarments would spoil the lines of the flowing silk of the skirt, and a bodice that might have once been reasonably demure would never be again. She knew exactly how the dress would look in the flattering glow of the antique chandeliers. For a half second her courage almost deserted her. But, she reasoned, if this worked, if she could reach Ben, she had far more to gain than to lose.

In an instant, allowing no time for a change of heart, the dress slithered over her like a second skin. A quick and careless brushing of her hair left it nearly as tousled as before. The glow of sun on her cheeks was all the blush required, and her lips were left kissably bare. A touch of mascara and a pair of sandals that were hardly more than a strap or two completed her costume.

"Ohh," she gasped, staring at the stranger in the mirror. "I look as if I just climbed out of some man's bed."

It was true. She knew it! She felt it! For the first time in her life she was as sexy as hell. Literally reeking of it. Exhilarated, determined to make the most of it, leaning closer to the mirror, she tried a come-hither smile. The result was startling in its success.

And again she pushed aside her doubts with a determined reminder. She was more than the last missing piece of his plan for Lainie. She was more than the young friend he'd known. She was a woman. If it took the foolish charade of a while ago and a scandalous dress to make the point, surely she could be forgiven.

Surely.

Not daring to risk her courage on a second look into the mirror, Victoria swept bravely from the room.

Ben was in the foyer as he said he'd be. He leaned indolently on the newel post. Laughter drifted from the garden, but he seemed not to hear as he stared into the distance, absorbed in his thoughts.

She waited at the top of the stairs, watching him, until with a canny awareness he lifted his eyes.

Still she waited, revealed yet half hidden on the darkened landing.

Blood left Ben's face in a rush. A half-smoked cigarette slipped unnoticed from his fingers. Only the sound of a tormented moan filled the taut silence.

Slowly Victoria stepped into a circle of light.

Seven

—

At first, in the pale light of the cut-glass chandelier, he thought she was naked, standing before him as she had countless times in memory and in dream.

"Oh, God." It was neither curse nor plea but the anguished benediction to a vision of loveliness. He could only wait, frozen in a heart-stopping timelessness, bewitched, wondering.

At the sound of his cry, Victoria moved. In unhurried magnificence she flowed sinuously from shadow to light like warm honey, and he saw she was clothed, indeed, from neck to knee in a sleek, simple gown.

It was soft and lustrous, its natural earthen tone blending with the warm glow of her sun-gilded flesh. Stunning in its simplicity, the gleaming fabric caressed her breasts, molding to her as smoothly as skin, fragile threads offering uncertain restraint for their fullness. A flaring skirt skimmed over slender hips, rippling and shimmering with each step.

Ben stood captivated as she took the steps one tread after another. A ghost from the past stirred, whispering a recollection of a painting and a dress of dark, lambent flame. But that was another time, an innocent time, long before the tropic days had bronzed her skin or maturity had blessed her body. There was nothing of that young innocence as she came to him now with her hair heavy and tousled about her face; her body a sweet, sensuous rhapsody; her eyes, light and golden, clinging to his.

At the last step, his gaze never breaking the bond with hers, he offered his hand. Her fingers closed strongly over his; her smile touched him like a kiss.

"You're lovely, Victoria." He drank in every inch of her like a man too long in the desert. There was a quietness about him, and an expression strangely like pain etched his face. His voice was low, so low she could almost have believed she imagined it. "Even lovelier than my dreams."

"Thank you, Ben," she responded, and in a secret part of herself she stored away the look and sound of him, one more treasure safely hers in the uncertain days ahead. She slid her hand through his arm and hugged it to her breast, gratified by the almost imperceptible tensing of his jaw.

"Is Jim here yet?" She allowed her body to sway against his as she looked up at him, her eyes lingering overly long in invitation on the taut line of his lips.

"He's been delayed for another hour or so. A minor emergency or something. Precious and Lainie are in the garden." He spoke mechanically, the words slurred, as if he neither knew nor cared what he said. "Precious decided we should take advantage of the coolness of the later hour and have dinner in the gaz-ebo."

"What a splendid idea. Dinner by moonlight would be wonderful. I've always loved moonlight." Through a veil of lashes she cast a hidden glance at him as she murmured, "I have cherished memories of it. Our memories."

"Don't!" The word was a guttural rumble as the last of his iron reserve crumbled. Desperate weeks of wanting, coveting, daring, then withdrawing de-stroyed his precarious self-discipline. A volcanic frus-tration exploded in him, magnified by her wanton teasing. From the depths of the torment that ravaged him rose a racking, bitter hurt.

A sound of agony hissed through clenched teeth. His arm jerked, pulling free of her caressing hold. In a slashing move his hands came down hard on her shoulders, his fingers biting into her like a vise. As he brought her against him, his face was grim, but his eyes held a wild hunger.

"You've never forgotten, have you, Ben?" Her voice was sultry, suggestive, and she wondered at her own sanity. It was sheer madness to speak of the night that had brought tragedy down around them. But de-spite the throb in her shoulders, something goaded her on. Something in her, some instinct, knew that an un-answered passion seethed within him like a gathering storm. She had claimed her *droit de l'amante*, her night of gentle, fulfilling love, and in her clumsy in-experience had sown the seed of bitterness. She longed now to set free the wild and soothe the bitter.

Perhaps Victoria could give what the princess had not. In a breath of a whisper she asked, "Can you ever forget?"

His muffled curse was as savage as the crush of his hands. His lips were rigid and thin. He looked as if he would never smile again. In a futile attempt at sanity he muttered, "You're playing with fire, princess."

He called her princess, not Victoria. Somehow she knew intuitively that he always would, and suddenly it no longer mattered. Not now. Not when he held her in his arms. Not when all she could think was how disturbing and provocative his chest was, pressing against her breasts with only the thin layer of shirt and gown separating them. Victoria wondered if she could really feel the roughness of his hair-covered chest against her sensitive nipples, or was it only a memory?

He was right, this was fire, and she wanted to be consumed. She was dizzy with her need for him.

"Maybe," she said as she touched him at the open throat of his shirt, stroking the pulsing hollow with her fingertips. "Just maybe I want to get burned."

"Then, damn you, you shall."

She was in his arms, swept against him by steel bands as strong as any prison. Light and shadow reeled about her as he climbed the stairs, and his breath was hot against her hair when she clung to him. His foot struck the door, destroying the fragile latch and antique hinges as it exploded inward. When he stepped inside and kicked it shut, its canted edges wedged and held, sealing them from the world as securely as the strongest lock.

He held her in the aftermath of silence, the rasp of his labored breathing a muted cadence, the spill of her silken skirt over his arms a curtain of bronze fire. His grip slackened, letting her legs swing free. Then slowly, ever so slowly, inch by sweet, agonizing inch, he slid her body down the length of his.

Blue eyes turned to molten gray burned into hers, searing her with the fury of desire. Her rising fear was vanquished only by the knowledge that this hurting, wounded man was her beloved Ben, once friend, always lover, if only in her dreams.

"Ben." She reached to stroke back his hair, seeking to pacify the fierce, untamed beast she'd unleashed. But he was beyond hearing, far beyond taming.

"Is this what you want?" His hands closed at her waist, clasping it in a curling claw of strength, drawing her closer, curving her body hard into his sinewy thighs. "This? This is desire. Desire and need, and wanting until it hurts. Do you know what it's like to live waiting and hoping? To be offered one small taste of paradise, then discover that's all it was ever meant to be? That you were an interlude—no more, no less?

"Do you know what it's like to wish desire would die, to will it to, and then find you've failed?"

She saw then that it was himself he fought; his anger was self-consuming. He despised the part of himself that succumbed to her, hated some dark secret. This was more than the friendship she'd destroyed, more even than Lainie. A demon rode him, one she didn't know. But she didn't have to know it to fight it with him, for him. Whatever it was he wanted, needed, she would give him. And now, deny it as he would, he wanted her.

Her hands were still at his hair, tangled at the nape of his neck. With a subtle pressure she drew his head down even as she rose on tiptoe to meet his lips with hers. "Ben, oh, Ben," she breathed against a mouth that was as unyielding as stone. Undaunted, she touched her tongue to the grim line in a darting flicker of lightning. Her body arched into his with natural ease, enticing, inviting, and she felt his groan against her mouth.

His big frame shook and his arms closed about her, enveloping her in a hard embrace. His mouth devoured hers and her lips parted in a shuddering gasp before the demand of it. The taste of him was spicy, faintly smoky, when the rough velvet of his tongue traced the smoothness of her lips, touching the straight edge of her teeth.

He stroked the taut curve of her back. In an exquisite caress his hand glided over her until the weight of her breasts rested in the joining well of thumb and palm, then it grew still. His mouth released hers, his head lifting just until his eyes could capture and hold hers. As he watched her, his thumb began a lazy foray over her breast, tantalizing a turgid nipple her dress did little to conceal.

Victoria shivered and closed her eyes, resisting the urge to turn into his palm, to seek the caress that would ease her aching breast. She waited desperately for the touch that never came.

"Look at me, Victoria." Her eyelids fluttered open, the blazing darkness of her gaze meeting his. "Tell me what you want."

"I want you," she said simply, with no attempt at artifice. "I want your kiss, your touch. I want—"

"Say my name," he demanded hoarsely. "Say it all."

"I want you, Benjamin Stockton." She said what he must hear and found no shame in meeting his need. "I want you now."

"Words!" he tried to scoff in a voice that broke. "As easy and meaningless as promises written on the wind."

Victoria wondered if he heard the torment of uncertainty betrayed in his taunt, and knew he hadn't. In a choice that had never been, one preordained when she'd taken that first step into the soft incandescence of the chandelier, her arms drew back from his shoulders and she stepped out of the circle of his embrace.

With a shaking hand she began to open the covered buttons that adorned her dress from neck to waist. They were tiny, her fingers clumsy. She moaned once in frustration as the last of the scalloped loops proved more stubborn than the rest. It was then that Ben brushed her hands aside and finished the task.

He smoothed her hair back from her neck and in one continuous motion slipped the yielding, diaphanous garment from her shoulders. In the fading light she was beautiful, standing in its drift of liquid gold as it fell in a pool about her feet.

For an unguarded instant she was vulnerable. As he drank in her beauty she made no effort to hide from him the naked yearning that only he could answer. She stood before him in trembling courage that surpassed pride. And he, who had sought to humble, was humbled himself by the complete trust she'd given. His heated arrogance, his compulsion to salvage his own pride, fled before her quiet calm. All was forgotten. She was again the enchantress who had once come to him in the first fall of darkness.

Barely suppressing a deep, shuddering groan, he reached for her. His hands curved about her neck, drawing her close. He was gentleness itself as he brought her bare body to his. "This was always between us," he said, his breath a rough melody against her hair, his passion a clarion against her nakedness. "Even when you were too young to understand."

Slowly she raised her head, brushing her lips lightly over his. "Yes," she said, "there was always this."

With his arm about her and her head on his shoulder he led her to the bed. Like gleaming topaz she lay on the creamy coverlet, watching, remembering, as he discarded his own clothing. Her arms were brown and strong as she lifted them to him, offering once more what he needed. "Ben Stockton, I want you."

Silently he came to her. His hands were gentle in her hair, his kiss soft on her lips, his mouth tender as he teased her breast, and when he found surcease in the temple that was her body, his silence was wondering. In fulfillment, he heard her call his name in ecstasy.

Then in repletion, holding her closely against him, he drifted with her into sleep.

Jim's faint shout of greeting followed by Lainie's delighted giggle woke her. Victoria stretched languidly, enjoying the pleasant ache that lay like a reminder in the pit of her womb. Smiling, she turned as naturally as life to the man at her side. Instead she found an empty coldness. Her eyes flew open, searching. She discovered Ben, fully dressed, standing over her, watching her.

"Ben." She said his name softy.

He made no response. Instead, in a hesitant, stilted motion, he cupped her cheek. With his thumb he brushed away a smudge of mascara that lay like a bruise beneath her eye. Once that wounded stain had been real. Tired, sick and desolate, she'd had nothing to sustain her but pride.

Tonight he'd asked it . . . no, demanded it . . . as sacrifice to his. And she'd given it to him, willingly. Now, in her eyes darkened by the passion they'd shared, there was serenity and a pride grown stronger. In that same golden darkness he saw reflected a contemptible man whose tarnished pride lay in tatters.

"You should hate me for what I've done," he said hoarsely.

"What?" Taken completely by surprise, she rose on one elbow, forgetting that she wore no clothing and unaware that the sheet slid from her shoulders to crumple about her waist. "I don't understand."

"I never meant for this to happen. Just as I never meant for it to happen eight years ago." Even in denial he longed to reach for her, to touch the fullness of her breast and linger to tease the rich, rose crest. A coil of disgust twisted his gut. "But damn my black heart, I did intend a part of it. I meant to hear you beg." His laugh was a sharp bark of derision. "If it gives you any satisfaction, retribution is far more painful than it is sweet."

In a rapid and startling change, he dropped his hand loosely to his side; his tone softened. "Tell Precious I'm sorry about dinner...that I remembered an appointment, one that couldn't wait."

By the time she gathered her scattered wits, the door slammed behind him. In an impossibly short time the engine of his car rumbled like thunder and gravel sprayed beneath the spin of tires.

Victoria slumped against the pillow, trembling and weak, her triumph turned to dust. What triumph was there in driving him too far? Driving him until, in an unthinking moment, he'd wanted to hurt her. She wondered now if she could ever forget his sickened look when he realized what he'd done.

Far the worst of it was that she'd seduced him. Again. And regret it as she might, it could never be recalled. Dully she wondered what she'd hoped to prove with this ill-fated fiasco.

It was an unnecessary question. She had wanted him to see her true self, and love her. She laughed, a humorless and bitter laugh. Ben had seen her, but not with love. Miserably she remembered his look of contempt, as if he hated her for making him want her.

Want. He had been right; it had always been there between them. Want, another word for lust. A word as empty. It was not enough.

Wearily, despondently, she rose and began to dress. Jim was there. Dinner would be soon. She must present herself, offer Ben's excuse, save face.

"Victoria?" Lainie waited in the open French door that led to the garden. A frown marred her look of youthful trust. "Did my daddy leave?"

Victoria pulled herself together and plastered a wide smile on her lips. "Yes, sweetheart. He suddenly remembered an appointment that couldn't wait."

"But he just got home. He always spends his first night home with me."

The disappointment that clouded her face cut Victoria to the quick. In her foolishness she'd caused Ben to hurt Lainie, the person who meant more to him than anything else in the world. Her only consolation was a promise that it would never happen again.

She took a dimpled hand in hers, saying with more assurance than she felt, "He'll be back. Probably before you know it. Now, I think we'd better join Jim and Precious in the garden. Are you hungry?"

"Starved as a crazy Indian." Lainie giggled and with the sturdy resilience of youth returned to her sunny nature. "I guess we'll have to save Daddy a midnight snack after all."

"Terrific idea."

"I get both drumsticks."

"You weren't supposed to remember that."

"Well—" Lainie giggled again "—if you're a good girl, I might give you one."

"After tonight, I promise to be the best girl anyone's ever seen."

Their laughter rose and floated on a breeze through the garden. One lighthearted and spontaneous. The other too gay, too forced, melancholy.

"Would you like to explain this evening to me?" Jim said into the prolonged silence, which was broken only by the chirping of a nearby cricket.

"I wish I could." Precious turned a worried countenance toward him as they sat alone over the remnants of a disastrous meal.

"The tension was so thick that it could have been cut with a knife. Even the little one felt it after a while," he grumbled as he leaned back heavily in his chair.

"She was disappointed. Her dad's never left her before on his first evening home."

"Did he mention this appointment earlier?"

"Not a word." Precious was emphatic.

"Could it be a woman?" Even as he asked it, Jim doubted.

"The only woman in Mr. Ben's life is Victoria," Precious answered in unshakable conviction.

"Do you think this appointment ever existed?"

"Not for a minute. In fact, I'd bet my best corset that he rushed through with his business to be home early."

"Then why the change of heart?"

"Something happened. When he came, Victoria and Lainie were having a marvelous time. We all were, and he joined in, even as tired as he was. He seemed happy just to be home. In fact, I thought..." Precious shook her head, then brushed aside what she'd meant to say. "Well, never mind what I thought. It doesn't matter anymore. What does matter is that between then and dinner, something went terribly wrong."

"Would they have quarreled?"

"No." The deep voice came from the shadows. A stone dislodged and rolled against another as a haggard and weary Ben stepped into the glow of the lanterns that lined the roof of the gazebo.

"We haven't quarreled." He stood before them, his hands hanging limply at his sides like those of a condemned man. His voice was roughened by strain. "I've been a monumental fool. I've come back to explain my stupidity and ask her, if she can, to forgive me."

"She went up to put Lainie to bed over a half hour ago and said something about turning in herself," Precious told him, her roving eye not missing the look of revulsion in his drawn expression.

"It's just as well," Ben said, unconsciously seeking the lighted room next to his own. "There're times when apologies are impossible. How can I ask her to forgive me when I can't forgive myself? This time I went beyond forgiveness. I tried to take from her something very precious—her pride—and instead lost my own honor. If she feels anything at all for me now except disgust, it would be pity. I couldn't face that."

"Now, now," Precious placated him. "Nothing could be that bad. You can talk with her tomorrow. It'll be all right. You'll see."

"My eternal optimist." Ben smiled a sad smile. "There are some things that even your determination can't fix."

Precious started to reply, but Jim's hand on her arm stopped her.

"Some things are better left unsaid, at least for now," Ben continued more to himself than to them. "I'll have to learn patience. If it's not too late."

"Patience and forgiveness often go hand in hand," Jim observed quietly.

"I can always hope." A broken breath rose and fell with the desolate statement. "Precious, I'm sorry about dinner, and Jim . . ."

"It's all right, Ben," Jim said to stop the tortured conciliation. "We understand."

"Do you?" Ben's question was no more than a sigh. "I wonder."

He turned on his heel abruptly before either Precious or Jim could respond. "I'll say good-night now. It's been a long day."

"Good night," his friends replied in unison, but Ben was already hidden beyond the shadows.

"They're tearing themselves apart," Jim said.

"Can we help?"

"I hear hope in your voice." He took Precious's rough hand in his and squeezed it. "You of all people should know that only they can resolve what's between them."

"At one time I feared the casualty in this would be Lainie," Precious said.

"But not now?"

"No. She'd accept Victoria as her mother right this minute with an open heart."

"Then it's Ben and Victoria? I can't believe they don't love each other."

"Just the opposite." Precious shook her coiffed head vehemently. "They love each other too well. Each is so afraid of hurting the other, of making an impossible demand, that neither is making a move of any sort."

"Ahh. I see," Jim rumbled in a low growl. "Then I'm afraid I might've complicated matters."

"How so?" Precious was eager in her search for a solution.

"I might've put impossible and, I suspect, unnecessary restrictions on Ben's conscience." He looked across the garden at a second light that now shone in the guesthouse bedrooms. "I'm beginning to think that maybe I misread the situation from the very beginning. Victoria was dangerously ill, but I shouldn't have discounted her strength."

Jim needed to make no further explanation. Precious understood completely. "Hmmpf!" she grunted. "Victoria's recovery's been complete for weeks, and still they're tiptoeing around each other, wearing their hearts, raw and bleeding, on their sleeves.

"What's needed is a good, old-fashioned case of selfishness. One or the other should just blurt it out plain and simple. I love you. So what're you going to do about it?"

"That's a bit drastic, wouldn't you say?" Jim said with a chuckle.

"I know, I know. But I'm not sure how many more nights like this I can stand."

"From the looks of both of them, I don't think they could stand many, either," Jim observed. "But all we can do is wait and pray they find their own solutions soon."

"Very soon." Precious sighed and refilled Jim's empty glass with lemonade.

* * *

Shrouded by the darkness of her room, Victoria stood before the open doors that led to the terrace. Leaning her head against the frame, she watched the moon set. The night had been long and sleepless. Guilt lay heavily on her heart in an endless ache.

The scratch of a match against a rough surface and then its glow muted by cupped hands was her only hint that Ben, too, had spent a restless night. She waited in the darkness as he stepped from his own room to the balustrade that overlooked the lake and the grounds of the castle.

Once, twice, he drew the cigarette to his lips, inhaling deeply each time. As he stared up at the building that rose against the graying horizon, he looked worn, exhausted beyond belief. Even the weight of his massive shoulders seemed more than he could bear.

Victoria felt like a voyeur, an intruder. It was painful to see a man of strength bowed under the force of his own private demons. She dared not move, yet knew she couldn't stay. Only the swaying hem of her nightgown stirred as she inched cautiously back.

"Stay. Please. If you can stomach my company." A muted, bitter laugh accompanied his words as he kept his back turned to her.

"You knew!" Victoria said in surprise.

"Your perfume. I'd know it anyplace, anytime. I remember..." He stopped, considered, continued. "It's the same?"

"It is." Victoria stepped onto the night-cooled stone of the terrace and was suddenly aware of scents that wafted on the summer breeze. Her own light fragrance blended and was lost in their sweetness.

"Strange, isn't it? Even among this profusion of flowers, yours is the one fragrance I'm aware of."

"Yes," Victoria agreed, wondering if he had read her mind. "Strange."

"Did you ever miss it?" Ben changed the subject adroitly, unexpectedly, but did not catch her off guard.

"No. I never missed the castle. The only happiness I ever knew was here, in the guesthouse." The admission was an oblique apology for her part in the disastrous evening, a gift that Ben seemed not to accept, for there was no response.

"I have to make a decision soon."

"About the castle?" she asked tonelessly as he relentlessly pursued the subject.

"It's been empty for too many years, Victoria. It's a crime not to give it the dignity of some usefulness. I've finally reached the point that I can staff it as it should be. Then Lainie can have all the things that go with such a background. No door will ever be closed to her."

Victoria stared at the hulking shadow, wishing she could explain to Ben and make him believe that the very things he wanted for Lainie would be the last to make her happy. But it was too soon; he would neither tolerate nor understand her intervention. Lainie had been his alone for too many years, and his dream for her had been part of his life for far too long. Victoria knew she couldn't change that in a day, or a week, or even months. But if she was patient, perhaps there would come a time when he would listen. For now she must keep her own counsel and hope.

"You'll burn yourself." Victoria stepped forward in sudden concern to flick the forgotten and smoldering cigarette from his fingers.

Her hand brushed his as she moved away. In a move like lightning he turned, tangling his fingers in her hair, holding her, tilting her face to his as if finally allowing himself the privilege of looking at her.

"You said that to me once before," he muttered, and the odor of brandy was strong on his breath.

"I remember," she said levelly, understanding at last the cause of his rambling.

"I burned myself, all right. Were you psychic? Did you know then that what we were to share was a night that would nearly destroy us all?"

"No, Ben. I was only young and foolish and selfish and rebellious. I gave no thought to anything. Not even to what I might be doing to Caroline."

"Couldn't you guess even then that once I'd known you I could never—" He stopped short and grimaced. His hold on her hair loosened; his arms dropped lifelessly to his sides. He withdrew from her as surely as if he'd walked away.

But Victoria was not to be denied. She would have her say. She stepped closer to him, unaware that her fragrance was more intoxicating than the oldest brandy. "I gave no more thought to that night than I did to tonight. You'd think twenty-six years would bring with them a bit of sense, but obviously they haven't. At least not where you're concerned."

"You didn't know that if you touched me I'd go up in flames?" Ben alluded mockingly to his loss of control.

"Neither that nor that I'd get burned in the process." Victoria made no attempt to deny complete knowledge of or responsibility for what she'd done.

"We both played with fire," Ben said heavily. "We both got burned."

"I'm sorry, Ben." Victoria wanted to put her arms about him, to comfort and be comforted.

She had no idea how beautiful she was in the dim light. Nor how desirable in a demure nightgown of gauzy cotton and lace. Ben was seized by the need to draw her with him through the beckoning doorway of his bedroom, to show her exactly what her touch did to him.

Reason, however late, warned that he mustn't. He knew he had, with his cruelty, lost that right. Perhaps forever. In his agony he searched for and found the faint evidence of bruises at her shoulders beneath the gown, and a sickness lurched viciously through him.

"It's cool, and you're not dressed for the night air." He allowed himself one quick caress of her satin cheek, a final crumb for a starving man. "Pneumonia's not something I'd like to add to my already overburdened conscience."

He drew a battered package of cigarettes from his pocket. "Go to bed, princess. Forget tonight ever happened."

He turned his back to her. Even as she obeyed, she heard the rasp of a match on stone and knew he'd moved beyond her reach.

Eight

————

The days that followed were comfortable and indolent, as the last of summer was apt to be. He was courteous and thoughtful, if aloof. The only time she saw evidence of his temper was in dealing with those who worked for him. Twice she heard him snarl into the telephone at some poor clerk who had the misfortune to deliver an irritating message.

Once she caught him staring at her in revulsion. Her first instinct was that he found her scarred fingers repulsive. Then common sense prevailed. The scars were well healed, invisible to all but the most probing inspection. It was the ugly but colorful bruises marking her shoulders that riveted him.

Before she could reassure him they weren't painful, he strode away, then cloistered himself in his study for the remainder of the day. She took to wearing only long-sleeved blouses and begged off when Lainie invited her to swim.

Yet for all her efforts, Ben moved grim-faced among them, remembering to smile only when Lainie or Precious teased him. The dinner hour grew quiet and morose. Ben began to find himself too busy to join them. Soon he found a reason to travel, his bag hardly unpacked before it was packed again.

Despite her concerns, Victoria saw that in his frenzied pace he remained the ultimate father. In his seeking of the finer things of life and breeding, there was not yet a hint of the erosive, unintended neglect that is so often ambition's companion. Time with Lainie was wedged between going and coming and followed by long days at his desk. If their hours together lacked, it was in quantity, not quality.

There were the odd moments when Ben would look up from a sheaf of papers and watch Victoria with an unfathomable expression. When their gazes met, she searched for some clue to why he wanted her there. Surely it was not to keep them in this painful limbo. Time and again she ached with the need to end this impasse, to ask what she could do to lift the troubled weight that crushed the laughter and contentment he'd known. She was struck mute by the fierce, impenetrable shell he'd built about himself, and it was a question she never dared ask. As quietly and unobtrusively as she could, she lived her life on the fringes of his.

In the empty hours of his absence and in his brooding presence, Victoria filled her time as best she could. Each day brought pleasure in her daughter and a closeness shared.

It was in the quiet hours between dusk and dawn that she yearned for Ben. Lying in her bed each morning after increasingly sleepless nights, she listened as he readied himself for his days at the office. Or listened, when he was away, for a step that never came. She missed as much as anything his breathy whistle, conspicuous by its absence.

As the days grew shorter and a hint of fall crept into evening, Victoria knew the time of reckoning was near. Nothing lasts forever, she chided herself, not happiness, not grief, not even indecision.

It was the philosophy that had helped her survive the tragedy and pain of her life and served, too, as a reminder that happy times must be lived to the fullest. As the days sped by, she clung to the hope that this knowledge would serve her as well in the future.

"Soon, Ben," she murmured to the rising sun as she stood on the empty terrace, clothed only in a robe. Her arms were folded about her against the early-morning chill. "Very soon one of us has to make a move."

As she waited for the full blaze of the sun, Victoria felt her own loneliness reflected in the fading darkness of the garden. Flowers drooped heavy-headed beneath the dew, but soon their petals would unfurl to the light and the garden would teem with life. She breathed deeply, filling her lungs with the fragrance of that life. Thoughtfully she turned away and crossed the terrace on bare feet. Mechanically she dressed in jeans and faded sweatshirt and tattered sneakers to begin her day. Then, pausing before the mirror, she bent to study the face of the troubled woman she'd become.

"Loneliness." Sad eyes looked intently into sad eyes. "Is it always the lot of a woman in love?"

Love? Have I ever admitted it so openly before? she wondered. "No," she answered her mirrored image, "never."

She spun about on the small stool, then walked, as in a trance, into the garden. Early fallen leaves bright with their autumn colors muted her footsteps, but she was blind and deaf to all about her. Her thoughts were on Ben.

She stopped and turned back, slipping her hands negligently into her jeans as she glanced dismissively over the castle. She turned to the guesthouse, that small sphere that had become her world. Lips that had been solemn lifted into a tender smile as her look touched on the room that was Lainie's.

"My beautiful little girl," she said as she'd never dared before. This was her day for courage, it seemed.

The smile faded as she looked at the closed and forbidding door of Ben's room. He was away again, but she didn't need his presence to see his rugged visage or to hear his voice. He lived within her. He was the beat of her heart, the breath in her lungs. His passion was the fire of her life, his gentleness her salvation.

"I love him."

The words were good. They healed the wound of loneliness. Suddenly she felt whole as she hadn't since the morning she'd left him that lifetime ago.

"I love him." She told the sky. She told the wind. She told the flowers about her. The words had dwelt in captivity forever. There was an exuberance in their freedom.

She would tell him. It would be the first step to heal the hurtful breach between them. Perhaps then she would understand what had gone so wrong in the aftermath of their lovemaking. Perhaps she would know what had hurt him so.

Her world was beautiful. Dew covered the garden in a glittering kaleidoscope, and the warm sun kissed her smiling lips. "I love him."

Ben was numb. He'd long since passed beyond exhaustion. For weeks he'd set himself a killing pace, hoping that a tired mind would be a tranquil mind. As he drove the last curving mile to the castle grounds, he knew he'd failed.

It was always the same. When he was with Victoria, he couldn't bear his misery or his self-imposed restraints or his disgust. And he would flee. Yet when he was away he fought his work like a maniac to rush home to Victoria. Only to flee again. It would be a joke, but no one was laughing.

The gate and its smiling guard loomed before him, and then the castle and then the guesthouse. In spite of everything, it was good to be home.

Ben stopped the car in the drive, thinking there would be time later to put it away in the carriage house converted to a garage. Loose gravel crunched under his feet; his jacket swung nonchalantly from the crook of a finger. His step was a little jaunty. It would be better this time. He'd make it be. They'd talk; he'd explain.

"Daddeee!"

The cry sent a shiver of cold dread down Ben's spine. He dropped the jacket into the dust as Lainie burst through a sparse hedge.

"Daddy! Daddy. It broke. She fell. She won't wake up." Lainie flung herself at her father as he bent to catch her. Her face, wet with tears, was buried in his shoulder.

"Shh, shh, baby. Calm down." He rocked her against him even as he instinctively examined her body for injuries. "Now tell me." He tilted her chin with a finger and looked into her frightened face. "Slowly and calmly. Tell me."

"The tree limb. It broke and she fell." She snuffled, and fresh tears spilled down her cheeks. "I tried and tried to wake her up, but she can't."

"Who, darling?" Ben asked in pretended calm.

"Vic . . . Victoria."

"When? Where?"

"Just now. At the tree house by the lake."

Ben's heart turned to heavy stone. Striving not to frighten Lainie more, he set her on the drive. "Lainie, listen carefully. Go to Precious. Tell her what's happened. Then wait for me in the house."

"Yes sir." Black curls bobbed as the child looked trustingly at him.

"Then scoot." Ben didn't wait to see if she obeyed. In three steps he vaulted the hedge and was running like a madman through shrubs and over flowers.

Once beyond the rose trellises he could see her, lying in a gaily colored heap at the base of a towering oak. A huge, jagged limb lay beside her, dwarfing her. A rivulet of red ran through her hair as it fanned out like silk over the grass.

He drew a rough breath as he knelt by her. She was so white, and still it was an instant before he believed she breathed. Sprawled as she was, there were no bones twisted at ghastly angles, no gaping wounds that spurted blood. There was only a swelling at her temple, coloring as he discovered it.

In anger and relief he slipped the band of vermilion from her forehead, stroking her with unsteady fingers. "Princess."

Her eyelashes fluttered as the warmth of his hands eased the sharp and jagged pain that streaked like a dagger through her skull. She focused blearily on him. "You're home."

"And not a minute too soon," he said gruffly.

"Some homecoming."

"Hush. Save your breath. Just nod to answer. Can you?"

Victoria nodded to prove it, and flinched with the movement of her head.

"Damn!" Ben exploded, and there was anguish in him for the pain. "I'm sorry, but I have to know. Can you feel your legs? Can you move them? Does your back hurt?"

"Just my head, Ben." In an effort to stem his torrent of questions, she opted to speak rather than move her head. "Lucky. The hardest place." She tried to laugh, and regretted the wave of nausea it brought.

Ben lifted her slender body, cradling her to him as he rose. In a gliding walk he moved as fast as he could without jarring her. Her head nestled under his chin; her damp forehead pressed against his chest; her lashes lay like delicate fans on her cheeks.

As Precious swung the door open for him, he had the sense of stepping back in time. "Is she hurt bad?"

"I don't know," he replied honestly, seeing his own worry reflected in her. "Call Jim."

"I did. Soon as Lainie told me. He's on his way."

Ben paused with his foot on the first step of the stairs. "Where's Lainie?"

"I sent her out to wait for Jim. It makes her feel better to think she's helping."

"Yes." Ben silently blessed this competent woman and was thankful for her insight.

"I'll get an ice pack for that bruise."

For some reason—he'd never know why—Ben chose to take her to his room instead of her own. He

placed her as easily as he could on the coarsely tex-
tured quilt that served as cover for his bed, then stood
looking down at her, feeling as he had many times before with Lainie. Relief that no horrible damage had
been done was swept away by anger at her foolishness. Only the frustration of his own helplessness sur-
mounted it. His face was a stern and forbidding mask,
his jaw a hard, craggy jut.

"You look like you'd like to hit something," Victoria murmured as she peered at him through lashes
that shielded her from the hurtful glare of the one
small lamp.

"I would," he snapped, and looked as dangerous as
an ill-tempered bear. "You. And I might just do it yet,
as soon as I know for certain you're all right." His
gaze slid over her and she shifted unconsciously before its arrogance. It was a mistake, one she couldn't
hide. He drew another angry breath as she paled and
trembled.

"What in blue blazes were you doing in that tree in
the first place?" he said in a muted snarl that she
knew, in Ben, meant a towering rage.

"Helping Lainie nail a loose board in her tree
house."

"You could've waited until I got home."

"I wanted to do it. My mother never concerned
herself with anything but keeping herself like a Dres-
den doll."

Mother. The word on her lips hit him like a batter-
ing ram. He recoiled from it in a paroxysm of remorse so intense that he felt weak. How many days
and weeks had he skirted about the issue, waiting?
Waiting for what... while she hurt and hungered for
her child. Mad with his own desires, he'd fled at every
opportunity, failing to recognize her distress. Was he

hell bent on hurting her? How many ways? How many times?

"I'm sorry I frightened you." Victoria was barely conscious now in her ramblings. "I only tried to be a good mother."

"God forgive me, you're not her mother. You never have been, and a foolhardy act like this can't change that," he snapped in bitter recrimination as the longing he heard touched a raw, bleeding nerve.

Victoria's hand clutched at the quilt, her knuckles straining against the threads. Barely lifting her head from the pillow, she stared at him, anger burning away the haze of pain. "How dare you!" she whispered. "Lainie is my child. She always was. She always will be, and nothing can change that. Not tragic misunderstandings or years of separation, not even a man too blind to—"

She stopped short. As quickly as it had come, her anger vanished. With a hopeless shrug that brought a wave of pain, she lay back on the bed. As she turned toward the wall and stared dry-eyed into emptiness, her soft, moaning sigh had nothing to do with her injuries.

"No. You don't understand. I didn't mean—"

"Never mind, Ben. It doesn't matter," she said tonelessly. "Just go away."

"Please, princess. Listen—"

"Not now, Ben," a soft voice of warning said behind him.

"Jim!" He looked desperately to the man who seemed to fill the room. "Help me. Tell her—"

"Not now, Ben," Jim said firmly. "You can tell her yourself later, and apologize. But right now, from the look of her, I'd say she's had about enough. Wait for me downstairs."

"But I have to tell her—"

"I said, wait downstairs, Ben."

It was an order, one Ben obeyed.

Jim had been gone for several hours. He'd checked Victoria, found no immediate problems, warned of concussion, prescribed a day of bed rest, refused dinner and said a reluctant goodbye.

As he sat alone in the gloom of his study, Ben wanted to go to her. He wanted to take her in his arms and promise he'd cut out his tongue if she asked it. But the grim warning that flashed in Jim's face had burned itself into his mind. Victoria had been through enough for one day.

"Daddy." Lainie hovered, subdued and uneasy, by his chair. "Are you busy?"

"Never too busy for you, sweetheart." He opened his arms and drew her onto his lap. "You were a very brave girl today. And smart."

"I was scared," she whispered against the strong beat of his heart.

"So was I. Being frightened's nothing to be ashamed of."

"I thought I made her get hurt."

"No, love." He added under his breath, "That's my specialty."

"But Daddy. You weren't even here with her," Lainie protested.

"I will be from now on, if she'll let me."

Lainie yawned and sighed sleepily, and Ben chuckled as her head grew heavier against him. "I know somebody who should be in bed. Would you like to pretend you're a very little girl again and let me carry you up the stairs?"

"Um-hmm. Can I kiss Victoria good-night? Just a tiny, little peck for sweet dreams?"

"Promise not to wake her?"

"Promise."

"Then why not? She could use some sweet dreams."

Lainie yawned again, hugely. "Will you kiss her, too?"

"I think I'd like that."

Long after Lainie was tucked in her bed and fast asleep, Ben paced the terrace. As was the custom when nights grew cooler, bedroom doors that led to the terrace were left open to the night air. His own was no exception, and the power of the woman who slept in his bed was strong. Tossing a newly lighted cigarette into the shrubs, he stalked through the door.

Victoria was snuggled beneath a cinnamon-brown sheet. Her hair was a glorious tumble over the pillow. She was honey and amber and topaz, a golden girl who was the sunrise of his life. He wanted to crawl into the bed with her, to hold her against him and feel her skin warm against his own. He wanted to give her his strength, to protect her.

"Who will protect her from me?" He laughed shortly and with no humor. "Who, other than me, is responsible for every unhappy thing that's happened to her?"

Cautiously he sat on the edge of the bed, hardly daring to breathe lest he waken her. A slight frown crossed her face; a whimper of pain pursed her lips. Ben winced and clenched his hands against the desire to comfort her. Instead he waited. Slowly she relaxed and slept untroubled.

She looked so right, there in his bed with her head on his pillow. He could almost see her as she would look tousled and warm from his caresses and radiant from a long night of leisurely loving.

He couldn't stop himself. He was tormented by a craving to touch her. Gently he brushed aside her hair, then leaned to press his lips to the ugly bruise at her temple. If he could he would draw all the pain and the hurt from it and from the deeper hurt he'd inflicted, as well.

Victoria moved restlessly; her hand closed tightly over his wrist. She mumbled something that sounded like his name. But when he looked at her, her lips were curled into a smile and he knew he'd been mistaken.

Her grip on his wrist showed no sign of relaxing. Ben tried to ease himself free. Her protest and the puzzled scowl that creased her forehead alarmed him. He stretched out carefully beside her, meaning to lie with her only until she released her grip.

From the look of her fragile body, she'd been a stranger to sleep and food of late. Tomorrow he would make what amends he could and see that she began to put back on the gorgeous pounds she'd lost. Tonight he'd see that she slept undisturbed.

It was Ben who slept. When he awoke, Victoria was gone.

Victoria's door stayed firmly closed the next day. From his study Ben watched as Precious and Lainie dashed up and down, moving freely in and out of her room.

Lainie seemed not to notice Ben's absence, but there were times when he felt the weight of Precious's puzzled gaze lingering as she passed by. He knew that all he had to do was close his own door, to shut himself away in his study and bury himself in his work, and he would at least escape her curiosity. But he couldn't. He found himself waiting, after each light knock, for Victoria's softly murmured invitation.

"What a mess. And every time I open my mouth, I make it worse." Ben pushed aside the papers on his desk. His taut, stiff fingers raked through his already disheveled hair. Wearily he buried his face in his hands.

"Mr. Ben?"

Ben looked up at Precious and tensed.

"Victoria's fine," she assured him hurriedly. "Her head aches some, and she's discovering muscles she never knew she had, but there's no sign of concussion. By tomorrow, except for the soreness and the fact that she'll sport a shiner for a while, she should be as good as new."

Precious saw the tension drain from him, but the distress remained. She suggested hopefully, "It might make you both feel better if you'd go up and see her."

"I'm the last person she'd see right now." He made no effort to hide the agony of the bleak admission.

"Trouble?" she asked.

"Of the worst kind."

"Can't it be put right?"

"I'm going to try, when she's stronger," Ben promised.

"Our Victoria's already strong."

"I know, but if she'll let me, I'll protect her, and nothing will ever hurt her again."

"That's not what she wants," Precious said emphatically. "She spent most of her young life being protected in the cruelest way. What she wants now is to be loved as the woman she is. If she has that, it'll be all the protection she'll need.

"Love her, Mr. Ben. That's all she asks. That's all she's ever asked." Precious paused and added, "She's loved you almost all her life."

Ben's head came up with a start in his surprise at Precious's blunt observation. "What?"

"She loved you long before Lainie was born."

"How could you know that? You weren't here then. Has she said it?"

"She didn't have to. Nobody did."

"Then how—"

"I know from Jim what a horror her childhood was. Think on it and tell me. Would the girl who wanted love more than anything else in the world have turned to any man but the one she loved?"

Ben's shoulders sagged wearily. "I know," he said softly. "I had finally begun to understand. I could see it in her face and in her eyes. But now, after today...

"Oh, God," he whispered, his fist clenched until Precious feared the bones would break. "What've I done?"

"I don't know," Precious answered honestly.

"How much, and how long can love survive?"

"Only Victoria can answer that."

"I think I can."

"Men!" Precious snorted loudly. In her uncommon exasperation her enormous breasts quivered like an earthquake as she abandoned all caution. "Will you ever learn not to do a woman's thinking for her? How do you know what that poor tyke's feeling lying up there all alone? For a man who didn't curse, I've heard you call God's name quite often lately. Now I wonder if you're not playing God.

"Or—" she paused for breath and a gleam of understanding shone in her expression "—are you afraid?"

"Precious!" Ben thundered, his skin dark and mottled with temper as she touched too closely to the truth.

"Don't Precious me. I'll have my say. You pussy-footed around one time and lost that girl." She glared down at him. "Are you going to sit around and do it again? So maybe you *will* lose her again! Shouldn't you go down trying, instead of failing because you tucked your tail between your legs and slunk off into the sunset?"

"Dammit—"

"What I should've done a long time ago was knock your heads together and make you both see the light. I might just do it yet," she threatened as she wheeled about in disgust. At the door a new thought occurred. "And don't try to fire me, for I won't go—and in case you haven't noticed, I'm bigger than you." The door slammed behind her.

His rage withered before the hope Precious offered. Maybe, he thought, just maybe she was right. She'd been uncanny in her judgments more times than he could remember.

"It's worth a try," he murmured. "For Victoria."

The sun was high the next morning when Victoria awoke. The terrace door was open, and the lazy noises of morning lulled her. She'd swung her feet to the floor, much to her regret, before she remembered her fall. A sharp, unsustained pain left a jagged trail through her brain. It was over almost before it had begun, and served only as a warning against sudden moves.

She stroked the peach-colored sheets and frowned. She could've sworn they were brown. But that was yesterday. Then she remembered the comfort of Ben's huge bed, waking at sunrise and finding his arms about her.

He'd been as blatantly masculine in sleep as in waking. With his shirt pulled awry, the thatch of dark hair that dusted his broad chest like a shadow had seemed an invitation for her fingers. The tangy, citrus scent of his cologne and the smokiness that lingered in his hair recalled a memory. With a sense of déjà vu, of another time, another dawn, and in spite of the hurts to mind and body, she wanted Ben Stockton more than ever.

She loved him. She'd desired him. But not until the ever-widening chasm between them was resolved. In the early-dawn light she'd fled his bed.

Now, pushing aside haunting thoughts, she engaged the problems of this day. The first hurdle was to see if her legs would support her. Gingerly she stood, and was pleasantly surprised. Except for the steel ball that bounced around in her skull at the inopportune moment, she felt as good as new.

"Well, almost," she grumbled as she caught sight of an eye and cheek that rivaled a dark rainbow. As she turned she discovered a vase of tiny wildflowers and a fold of fine cream bond that lay beside it. Her name across it was a slash in the blackest ink. Ben's writing hadn't changed. It had been bold and arrogant and imperious even when he hadn't been. As she read the curt message she marveled at how strong an indication his handwriting had been of the man he had become.

She'd been summoned to his study, tersely, and with only the preamble "when you're up to it." Her heart began to pound with an uneven rhythm, and the strength of legs she'd been so proud of threatened to desert her. Yet she knew delay would only make it worse. With a last check in the mirror and a sigh over her appearance, she left her room.

As she reached the last step, Precious rose from a small table and called her to the telephone. "Telephone? For me? Nobody ever calls me," she protested.

"Well, maybe nobody did, but a Mr. Roarke Cassidy has," Precious drawled.

"Roarke!" Ben's note dropped unnoticed from her hand as she raced to take the receiver from Precious. "Roarke," she cried again, and began to speak in breathless snatches. "You're here? In the States? In the village! My letter about Lainie? But you shouldn't have! Of course I'm desperate to see you. How soon can you be here? Twenty minutes?"

Then she laughed, an eager impatience in her lilting tone. "I know you can't fly. I know. I know. You don't have wings. Yet.

"But hurry, please. I'll be waiting. I need you, Roarke." Victoria dropped the receiver in its cradle with a clatter. She was smiling as she turned and found Ben watching her from the study doorway. In her excitement the hurt and anger between them was forgotten; she wanted only to share her pleasure, to tell him of Roarke. "Ben, you heard?"

"I heard."

"I can hardly wait for you to meet—"

"Not now, Victoria," he interrupted her grimly. There was a harsh element of anger beneath cool irritation as he glanced down at his watch. "I'm a bit too busy for conversation."

"But your note! I thought you wanted to talk!"

"Perhaps I did, but I've discovered I really don't have the time to listen to your chatter."

"Chatter!"

"Yes, chatter," he snapped, and as Victoria watched, speechless in astonishment, he walked away.

Roarke Cassidy arrived at the castle in less than the proposed time. As he watched in a nasty frame of mind from the safe distance of his study, Ben wondered if the man hadn't sprouted wings after all.

The dusty, battered vehicle of obscure origin had drawn to a screeching halt before the guesthouse. A dark, heavy-shouldered man unfolded his incredible length from under the steering wheel just in time to catch a laughing Victoria in a whirling embrace.

Ben strained to hear as they walked arm in arm over the drive. In their happy eagerness their words tumbled over one another, making no sense to any but them.

"Your letter was a kick in the gut."

"For me, too..."

"That's quite an eye..."

"It's not what you're thinking."

"It'd better not be."

"Roarke, he wouldn't!"

"How's the little one?"

"Beautiful! The most beautiful child you've ever..."

"...send their love."

"I miss..."

"Can you stay?" Victoria's clear voice penetrated Ben's tumbled thoughts.

"For a night, maybe two." The deep cadence held a fascinating serenity, if Ben had been listening to more than the hated words.

"No more?" Victoria said mournfully.

"Sorry, Missy. It's the best I can do."

"Then come and meet... my family."

Ben heard Victoria's knock. No matter how little he wished to answer, he knew he must. His steps were heavy as he crossed to open the door.

"Ben." If speech could hold a smile, Victoria's did. "This is a very special friend from Purgatory, Roarke Cassidy."

Ben wondered how many times he'd heard that name in the past half hour. He liked it less each time.

The man, dressed in jeans and shirt that were as disreputable as the duffel he carried, slipped his arms from Victoria's shoulders and offered his hand with a grin.

Ben had to look up at him, so far that his neck ached as he stared into a countenance that would have done justice to the silver screen. Disheveled lustrous black hair fell over a high, wide forehead and strong brows. Fair skin and sky-blue eyes fringed by incredible lashes were saved from pure beauty by the sheer, chiseled strength of his jaw and chin.

If Ben had doubted the ruggedness of this man, it was there in the burly size and in the rough callused hand he ignored. Something seemed to explode inside Ben as he glared up at this Adonis.

"Mr. Cassidy," he said curtly, and nodded in acknowledgment, his only concession to civility. "I'm sure Victoria will see to your comfort. Now, if you'll excuse me, I do have work to do."

Victoria gasped as Ben shut the door in their faces. She looked in confusion at Roarke. "I'm sorry. Ben's been like this with me for days, but I didn't expect him to be this way with anyone else. I don't know what's gotten into him."

"I think I do," Roarke said in his deep rumble, then smiled again as he bent to retrieve his duffel. "Now why don't you show me to a room so I can clean up a bit."

Nine

A boom of unrestrained laughter filled the morning, harmonizing with Precious's rich chuckle and Lainie's descant trill. The sound brought Victoria completely and happily awake. Roarke! He was here. And as he had once before, he would take her troubled life in his two big gentle hands and set it aright. That certainty brought a smile to her lips as she tossed the covers aside and dashed for a bath.

In her haste she didn't knock. The sight of Ben, nearly naked and damp from the shower, halted her flight. He was aggressively handsome, clad in a slash of color she dimly recognized as a towel. Her startled eyes glanced off the cool blue of his, unable to hold his gaze.

The silence was explosive. A shackling stillness magnified every breath, the flutter of an eye, even the beat of her heart. Something as volatile and turbulent as the fury in his passed between them and left her trembling.

In the smothering vacuum Ben laid his razor aside, breaking Victoria's mesmerized trance. A blush tinted chalk to crimson as she realized she'd been staring, fascinated by the broad expanse of his chest and the smooth striation of sinew and bone beneath bronzed skin.

She knew the corded muscles of stomach and waist would be rock hard to her touch. After years at a desk, he had the trim perfection of the athlete he'd been. Her heart admitted what her mind had denied. Despite the misunderstandings, the cruelty and the anguish, she wanted his strength, needed it, bone, sinew and muscle under her adoring hand. Shaken, she rushed into a babbling apology. "I didn't expect you. You're usually gone before now."

His gaze traveled from sleep-tossed hair to bare toes that peeped from the hem of her gown. She was clean and scrubbed and clothed. Chaste in her simplicity. Yet a possessive anger flashed over him, the lines about his mouth hardening into stark unforgiving brackets. "I overslept this morning." His voice was a grave mutter. "I was a while getting to sleep last night."

Victoria was instantly contrite as she saw the ravages of an unrestful night. "I'm sorry. I imagine Roarke and I are at fault. We had so much to catch up on that we lost track of time. I don't know when we—"

"It was three thirty-four," Ben interrupted her roughly.

"I had no idea. I'm sorry."

"Blast it! Quit apologizing. You're a grown woman. If an old love chooses to visit you, it's no affair of mine." The thunderous look on his face declared differently, but Victoria was too stunned to see.

"Old love?"

"Yes! Old. He's forty if he's a day, too old for you."

"Roarke's thirty-nine, and he's not . . ."

Ben jerked the towel from his waist and sent it flying into a heap. Splendidly naked, he wheeled about. "Be my guest, Victoria. The bathroom's all yours. I'll shave at the office."

"You're jealous!" she burst out in barely contained shock, oblivious, for once, of his body.

"Damned straight," he agreed, and slammed the door behind him with such force it should have destroyed hinge and latch. Victoria was left staring openmouthed. It wasn't until she heard the roar of his car leaving the driveway that she managed to gather her scattered wits.

As she slipped into jeans and shirt, her attention was drawn to the inevitable bouquet of fresh wildflowers that were a part of every day. Confusion was forgotten as she touched the velvet petal of a tiny flower as bright as her daughter's smile. "Thank you, Lainie."

Victoria's smile faded; an uncertain world intruded. With a heavy step she turned away, forcing herself to walk when she wanted to run—run to Roarke, a source of strength.

A day whose beginning had been less than auspicious spun away into a peaceful afternoon. Victoria and Lainie and Roarke whiled the hours away by the pool. Roarke soothed Victoria, delighted Lainie, and put the world back in kilter. If there were undercurrents of tension, they remained below the surface, where he intended they should. At least for now.

Victoria and Lainie were involved in a noisy race across the pool when Roarke heard an approaching engine. He promptly excused himself, then wandered away. It was time to set the stage for his private drama.

"Precious, my sweet. Do you think I could have another brownie? They're so delicious, they're almost sinful." Roarke's tone was teasing, filled with laughter as he stepped into the kitchen brightened by the late-afternoon sun.

"And it's sure I am you've kissed the stone," Precious retorted cheerfully.

"It's true my blood runs pure black Irish, but there's not a bit o' the blarney on my lips." Roarke snagged a brownie, flashing a smile guaranteed to send even the most stolid heart into flutters.

"A little on the tall side to be Irish, aren't you, Cassidy?" A hard voice cut like a rapier through the light banter. "Even a second generation Irish American." Briefcase in hand and loosened tie askew, Ben loomed in the hallway, grim and rigidly unamused.

"It's first generation instead of second," Roarke corrected him mildly.

Ben swept Roarke with a glare that grew colder. He waited, tense, watchful. He had the look of a ruffian spoiling for a fight. Anything Irish was an endangered species.

"Ahh! For my sins!" Roarke rolled his eyes heavenward. Despite his gentle nature and years of self-denial, he liked nothing better than a good donnybrook. Brawling had been the bane and the joy of his existence. No one asked for it more than Ben Stockton, but it didn't fit Roarke's plan. Regretfully he ignored the unspoken challenge.

"The tall Irishman's not unheard of," he said pleasantly. "We're throwbacks, the result of the joyful pillage of some Viking raider." Deliberately placing two more brownies on a napkin, he looked again at Ben. "Missy and Lainie and I are picnicking by the pool. Care to join us?"

"No, I wouldn't," Ben said tautly.

Another man might have been intimidated by the icy contempt. Any man but Roarke, whose smile was angelic, his manner sympathetic. "Too bad. I don't suppose you'd like to come out to dinner with us, either."

"No," Ben snapped. He wavered, poised like a wary brigand, then in impotent anger he stalked away.

"He doesn't know," Precious said in surprise.

"Hasn't a clue," Roarke agreed as he let the secret vigilance of his big body relax.

"How did that little omission occur?"

"He was just a little too disturbed to listen to proper introductions."

"They've both been disturbed for weeks." Precious sighed.

"I know, but it won't be long now."

"I thought that weeks ago, too."

"Ahh. But the padre wasn't here weeks ago."

"That's true." Precious chuckled dryly. "I believe you're a leprechaun in giant's clothing."

"Perhaps I missed my calling. Do you think it would suit me to wear a pointed hat and spend my life revealing treasures to poor misguided souls?"

"Don't fish for compliments. You're a handsome devil, and you know it."

"Precious, my dear friend, if I'd met you years ago, my life might've taken a different direction," Roarke teased.

"Certainly. When you were in short pants and I was already a woman grown." Precious stifled a grin and handed him the brownies. "Here. Hush with your nonsense. We both know your work's your life. So take these out to my girls and cross your fingers that someone around here gets some sense in his thick head before it's too late."

"I suspect tomorrow will tell the tale."

Precious slanted him a suspicious glance. "What mischief do you have up that black sleeve of yours?"

"Not a thing," Roarke insisted with exaggerated innocence. "Things will simply take their natural course."

"With a little assistance from you?"

"Well, maybe a little."

"Then you'd best enjoy the brownies while you still have teeth."

"Good idea." Roarke laughed as he left the kitchen, looking not the least worried about his teeth.

In the early morning the dark hush of the guest-house was suddenly alive with a rush of disparate sounds. From the end of a small hall a grandfather clock struck shortly the wee hour. In the drive the hollow metallic thud of a car door was followed by an indistinct rumble from Roarke. Victoria's happy laughter rose to join in, filtering through the garden as sweet as the song of a nightingale. Then, like the falling of the last domino, a low curse from the study was muffled by the shattering of glass.

As quickly as it had come, the furor ended. The clock ticked quietly toward the new hour; laughter dwindled. There was only black silence from the study.

Dressed as was his custom in jeans and a faded T-shirt and showing no ill effects of his late night, Roarke had just descended the stairs when the study door was flung open. Disheveled and hostile, Ben stared with a hard, determined sneer into mild eyes that were bluer than his own.

"Rough night," Roarke observed in sympathy.

"It's time you left, Cassidy," Ben declared without preamble.

The bigger man studied him carefully, not missing the strained readiness of his guarded posture. Unintimidated, he nodded affably. "I think perhaps you're right."

"She's not going with you."

Roarke paused in the act of turning to reclimb the stairs, and Ben was startled by his look of pity. "What made you think she would?" His eyes seemed to bore into Ben's. "You're a fool, Ben Stockton. But the fool she wants, and that's what counts.

"I'll go pack now, but before I leave we'll have a little talk." Roarke swung about nimbly and began to retrace his steps.

Ben looked after him, feeling not a shred of triumph. He began to suspect he'd been a fool indeed. "So. What else is new?" he asked under his breath as he returned to his study. "All that remains now is to find out how, and how great. Which I'm sure Mr. Cassidy will take roaring delight in informing me."

Ben had splashed himself with cold water in the bath off the study and was back at his desk, looking only a trifle more refreshed, when Roarke's knock battered at the door—a farcical observance of formality, for in the next instant he entered. Ben looked up from his aimless shuffling of files.

"Oh, my God!" Papers scattered as they slipped through stunned fingers.

"Sorry, but no," Roarke returned cheerfully. "Merely his faithful servant."

Ben sat speechless as Roarke dropped his duffel by a chair. As he straightened, the light shone on the heavy cross falling over white collar and black vest.

"I didn't know," Ben finally managed.

"You've made that patently obvious."

"I suppose I should call you father."

Roarke chuckled. "Let's strike a bargain. If you won't, I promise not to call you my son."

A smile broke over Ben's bemused features as he relaxed and leaned back. "You've got yourself a deal."

"I thought I might."

"It's too bad we couldn't have settled our earlier differences as easily."

"What differences?" Roarke's smile was cherubic.

"I can see that it doesn't pay to argue with a man of the cloth."

"I have help." The rugged visage beneath a shock of black hair was deadpan, but laughter lurked wickedly.

"I give up." Ben sighed. "So why don't you make your victory complete and sit down and go into detail about what a fool I've been."

"A lucky fool."

"Let's hope so," Ben said, a touch of worry flitting over his features. "How much a fool is a man allowed to be?"

Roarke made no effort to answer as he eased into a chair opposite Ben. "What would you like to know?"

"Everything. From beginning to end."

"All right," Roarke agreed, seeing the thirst in him. "It all began in a little church for derelicts on the waterfront in Savannah."

"Savannah! That's hundreds of miles away." Ben interjected, but Roarke took no notice.

"I was home on sabbatical and filling in a few days for a friend, a street priest who works in the worst parts of the city. The poor souls who passed through his parish were a pitiful, transient lot. Then one day Victoria was there. Lost and desperate, but as beautiful as a ray of sunlight. She was hardly more than a child, but her eyes were old and empty. At the tender age of nineteen, she had no future. Life was something to be endured."

Ben stifled a strangled groan.

"I did what little I could for her in my short sojourn there, but it was too little. She was a shattered jewel wandering those dark, dank alleys. She didn't belong. The street would've destroyed her. I couldn't allow it. I couldn't leave her," Roarke said simply.

"You took her with you." There was relief and gratitude in Ben's words.

"I took her with me to South America, a companion for my sister, the very lonely bride of the plantation's manager. Victoria took to the life and the hardships as if it were her second incarnation. Before long she was helping in the hospital, and when she showed a natural ability with the women and children, she was trained as midwife.

"We'd worked together for years before she told me about her baby. It was the answer to a great number of questions."

"Her hands!" Ben raised tortured eyes to Roarke's. "Tell me what happened to her hands."

The fury that slashed across Roarke's compassionate face was shocking. His voice became a snarl. "It seems to be the fashion for every small country to have its own self-styled bandido. We were no exception.

Ours was a bandy-legged creature who fancied himself a great leader. For the most part he'd been little more than a nuisance, until he called for Victoria to help his wife.

"At least he called her his wife. She was likely some poor peasant child stolen from her family and forced to be his..." Roarke stopped, his lips a taut white line. After drawing a deep breath, he continued. "His concern was all show."

"But Victoria went?"

"Yes. She went unprotected into the hills and did her best. Though nothing could've helped the poor starved, overworked child, our great general wouldn't believe it. He had to blame someone."

"Victoria," Ben said quietly.

"Of course. While the idiot was beating his breast in a show of grief, she managed to slip away and make a run for it back to the village. He demanded we give her to him as a replacement. When we refused, he burned the hospital."

"She burned her hands then?" Ben's voice was like nothing Roarke had ever heard.

"There's a small boy with the smile of an angel who'll grow to be a fine man because of those scars. She plucked him out of a burning hut as coolly as an angel herself. She was dreadfully hurt," Roarke said solemnly. "Our supplies were devastated, and our missy witch doctor had become a threat to the village. Every man, woman and child would've fought for her, but she wouldn't allow it. Instead, to avoid more death and destruction, she chose to leave us."

"When she was half out of her mind with fever she called herself witch doctor." Ben spoke of trivia, unable to deal with the danger.

"A silly name I gave her." The dark look on Roarke's face lifted; a smile tilted a corner of his mouth. "It caught the natives' fancy and became her title of respect."

"She's quite a woman."

"She is that. We'll all miss her. At one time we'd hoped someday she'd come back to us."

"Where was she going in the meantime?"

"To begin formal training at a teaching hospital in the Midwest. Instead, she found her child."

"And you came hundreds of miles to make sure she was all right."

Roarke didn't bother to deny it. Instead he asked, "Wouldn't you?"

"Anywhere, anytime. On my knees, if need be," Ben said huskily.

Roarke sighed and inclined his shaggy head in satisfaction. He rose to his feet. "I'll be going now."

"Will you say goodbye to Victoria?" Ben rose, too, and stood looking with new perspective at this Irish giant.

"She had a long night. When I looked in on her she was sleeping, so I left a note on her pillow. With luck she'll sleep most of the day." He paused and grinned. "I'll be back."

"I hope so," Ben said as he offered his hand.

Roarke's hand dwarfed Ben's in a grip that was firm but not crushing. He held it longer than was usual. "I've told her that you love her."

Ben wasted no time in wondering if he'd been that obvious. "I do. I always have."

"A woman always likes to hear it for herself."

"I know. It's a mistake I made once, but not again."

"The night Lainie was conceived?"

"It took eight long years, but at last I understand."

"You know, then?"

"That Victoria loved me?" Ben's face showed nothing; only his shadowed eyes betrayed him. "I know now that she did...then. Lainie was a child of love."

"It's as it should be," Roarke agreed, offering no comment. The future he would leave in their capable hands.

"When will we see you again?"

"Why, at the wedding, of course." The booming laugh echoed through the room. "Did you think I'd miss that?"

Ben laughed in answer and it held a hint of dreams and hope. "Somehow, I didn't think you would."

Only three waited in the drive to wave a final goodbye. Swinging his agile body into the incongruously small seat of the car, Roarke scanned the quiet building beyond them where Victoria slept the first peaceful sleep she'd known in weeks. A look of pleasure shone on his mobile face as his gaze flicked over Ben and the child by his side. With a grinding of gears, a wink for Lainie and a jaunty wave, he drove away, leaving behind a sense of peace and a cloud of dust.

When Victoria awoke, she required no clock to tell her she'd slept the day away. She knew by the refreshed contentment that dispelled the weariness in her bones and by the shadows that crept into her room. She stretched luxuriously and realized that she was ravenous. Her grateful gaze discovered a plate of sandwiches and a cooler left by Precious. With greedy inelegance she bounded from her bed.

After she'd eaten with hearty appetite, then dressed, she extracted from the folds of her tangled bedcovers the white envelope that had slipped from her pillow. She'd known it was there. She didn't need to look at the bold script to know whose hand had held the pen. She knew instinctively what it would say. She wanted to walk among the flowers. In the solitude of the garden she would say her goodbye to Roarke.

Her telephone jangled; she reached for it. "Hello." Sleep had left her voice sultry. A hollow silence was her answer. "Is anyone there?"

"Princess."

"Ben! Good morning, or should I say good evening?"

"Did I wake you?"

"No." She laughed. "I was awake, but only just."

"We have to talk." There was a desperation in him.

"I know."

"I'm in a board meeting, or I should be. I ducked out for a minute. It's been going on for hours, and it looks as if it might go on forever."

"I'll wait for you." She asked wistfully, "Forever, did you say?"

"Princess." He hesitated. "No, never mind. It's waited this long; it'll keep a few more hours." There was a click and he was gone.

Much later, surrounded by the fading splendor of Indian summer, Victoria sat on the grass, the note in her hand, lost in a time that would never come again. She had no idea how long it was before she realized that the soft mewling she heard was not a tiny animal secreted in the shrubs.

Rising to her feet and sliding Roarke's note into the pocket of her jeans, she followed the winding path to the stream that fed the lake. A carpet of pine needles cushioned her step. The undergrowth was thick; a wall of green muffled the cries. Victoria stopped, listened, unsure of the source. Then, as she stepped into a small glen, the cry was as clear as the crystal water. It was Lainie's.

Victoria's heart lurched in fear, but the whimper was not one of pain. Lainie was upset, but unharmed. "Lainie," she called quietly in an effort not to startle the child. "Darling, can I help?"

Lainie looked up at her from her perch on a great outcropping of stone that jutted over the creek bed. Her eyes were huge. Tears glistened in them like topaz. Dirt streaked her cheeks, and in her grubby hand she clutched a cluster of drooping, ugly stems. Fresh tears welled on her lashes.

"They blew away." She snuffled. "I picked you some pretty flowers that looked like lace and they blew away."

Victoria moved to the distraught child and sank beside her. Gently she drew her into her arms. She understood. Lainie had picked dandelions that had been heavy with seed. An errant breeze or their own heavy ripeness had cast them adrift.

"Shh, shh," she comforted her child. "It doesn't matter. We'll find others."

"But these were special," Lainie sobbed against Victoria's breast.

"All the flowers you've been leaving in my room were pretty. I like wildflowers best of all."

"I like the little ones that hide in the grass." Lainie scrubbed at her cheeks with the back of her hand, smearing dirt into a long streak of mud.

"I never saw you put the bouquets in my room, but I always knew it was you." Victoria brushed a damp curl back from her forehead and kissed her lightly.

"Tommy Barton said that his daddy left them because he didn't like bad little boys. Tommy and Timmy made him sad. I thought the flowers would make you happy and you'd stay."

"You've been awfully quiet lately, Lainie. Was that why? Were you afraid I'd leave?"

Lainie nodded vigorously. "I tried to be still as a mouse and be a good girl. Then you might love us enough to never go away."

Tears she dared not shed lay heavy and threatening behind Victoria's eyes. She distrusted her voice, but she had to ask. "Do you truly want me to stay, Lainie?"

"More than anything." A small hand crept into Victoria's. "You make us laugh. Sometimes even Daddy."

"You make me laugh, too," Victoria said as she caressed the dark head that had begun to droop against her. "I've never been as happy as I have since I met you."

"You could marry my daddy. Then you would be my mommy and never, ever have to leave again," Lainie suggested gravely, then yawned hugely, exhausted by her tears.

"I don't know about the marrying part, sweetheart." Victoria rocked to and fro, cuddling the child against her. "But I promise I'll never go away."

Lainie wriggled against her. "Cross your heart?"

"Cross my heart. No matter what, I'll never leave you." She buried her lips in the black curls beneath her chin. "Not ever again," she murmured so inaudibly that the child couldn't hear.

Lainie yawned again and Victoria chuckled. "Someone I know should have a bath and go straight to bed."

"Daddy helps me when I'm very dirty." Lainie held out a hand that qualified.

"Would you like me to do it this time?"

A nod was her answer. "You could tuck me in and read me a story." A serious face lifted to Victoria's. "We could pretend you're my mother back from a long, long trip."

Victoria bit her lip to silence a startled gasp. But when she searched the trusting eyes, she found only innocence. She had no idea that tears were streaming down her face until Lainie lifted a dimpled finger to wipe a drop away.

"Did I make you sad?"

"No, my darling. When you're older you'll understand that sometimes tears are happy." She managed a tremulous smile. "Are you ready now for that bath?"

"And a story? And a good-night kiss?"

"There's nothing in this world I'd like better."

Twilight cast long shadows behind them as they walked hand in hand through the garden.

Ten

The night was wine dark. Victoria stood on the terrace, listening. The haunting wail of an owl rose from the forest; a whippoorwill cried by the lake. From the darkness behind her a footfall sounded.

"Lonely sounds, aren't they." Ben stepped from the gloom of an overhanging oak.

"Yes." Victoria didn't turn as she kept her hands palms down on the rough stone of the balustrade.

"Will you miss him?"

"Roarke?" She tilted her head, her hair swinging in an aura of fragrance. "I'll always miss him. I owe him my life."

"I know," Ben said. "I tried to thank him, but he wouldn't listen."

Victoria laughed, a low madrigal, but said nothing. Ben longed to see her face, to read what message her eyes might hold. "Princess." His voice was a rasp.

"I'm sorry. I've died a thousand deaths each time I've seen the hurt in you. I'll do anything if you'll forgive..."

Her smile swept his remorse away as she spun toward him. She took a step forward as the moon broke free from a drifting cloud. She wore only his shirt; her legs were bare beyond its hem. "Sweet idiot." She laughed again, and its music surrounded him. "Did you rehearse that pretty speech?"

"No." He hesitated. His flashing eyes met hers, and he laughed, too. "Yes, I did, with each of the thousand deaths."

"I don't want your apologies, darling. No more than Roarke wanted your thanks."

His body tautened at the endearment. He had to restrain himself from catching her up in his arms, but caution dictated patience. Their path was strewn with too many mistakes to rush headlong into another disaster. His eyes searched hers. "What do you want?"

"Don't you remember?" She swayed toward him. Fingers brushed his chest, lingered, caressed. "I told you years ago. I want what the other girls want when they come to you."

"There are no others," he said. Her touch was a flame, fierce and burning, in his blood.

"Ahh." The sigh was a satisfied purr. "How unfortunate for them."

"No games, princess. I've told you I don't play."

"And neither do I."

"Do you know what you're doing?" His hands lifted of their own volition, closing over her shoulders.

"Do you know what I'm doing?" With her thumbs touching, she ran her palms over the thin fabric of his shirt. The wiry curls beneath were rough to her fingertips.

"I'm not sure," he admitted, then shuddered as she traced the line of his shoulders, caressing the hard muscles from forearm to wrist. Her hands rested over his at her own shoulders, then drifted down until her arms were over her breasts.

Her fingers lay at the lapels of her shirt's deep-plunging neckline. She looked down as she crumpled the clinging fabric and lifted it away from her body. Slowly, ever so slowly, she raised her face to his.

There was invitation in her eyes, but what did it really mean? Ghostly memories haunted him. Years of loneliness, of pain and disillusion, of mistakes and trying to hate, of cruelty and of loving, had wreaked havoc. But the stronger was love. A love he must not let blind him. There was torment in the harshness of his tone but hope in his eyes as he muttered again, "I'm not sure."

"Then let me show you." One button after another slipped from its mooring under her slim fingers until the shirt hung free, touching her only at shoulder and neck and taut nipple. Ben glimpsed her naked, half-hidden golden flesh.

"Do you mean this, Victoria?"

"Do I mean to seduce you?" She sighed and the shirt fell away from one breast, revealing a perfect body. "I've waited a lifetime for it."

"A lifetime." His voice, as soft as the night air, was a low, ragged throb. "A lifetime is what it'll be if I take you now. This time means forever. You'll be mine. There'll be no going back. If you leave me, I'll find you. You'll never escape me." He paused. The breath he drew seemed to tear from his lungs; his eyes seared her with their burning intensity. "If you don't mean this, if you don't understand that we're going to belong together forever, walk away, Victoria. Finish it now, before it's too late, or it'll never be finished.''

"It's already too late." She looked at him steadily. "It's been too late since I was eighteen. It began then and it never ended. I wanted you then; I want you now. I'll always want you."

"After all I've done? How can you? I took your innocence and stepped out of your life. I hated you. I made you beg. With my clumsy tongue I've hurt you time and again."

She stopped him with a finger against his lips. "You never meant to hurt me. Never. You didn't take my innocence. I thrust it at you in a useless rebellion. You didn't make me beg. You needed the words. Because you thought that I once cared so little for you that I offered your child to another man, you needed..." Her voice faltered, trembling. She cupped his jaw with her hands. "It was never that, Ben. Oh, God! It was never that."

"Then tell me, Victoria. Help me understand." He wondered if that strange, croaking voice was his.

"Because you never really wanted me, I couldn't trap you with a child. I had promised no ties to bind you." She said it simply, honestly, and a knife twisted in him.

He made no reply; he couldn't. He choked on grief for the girl who'd known so little love that she hadn't recognized it. But soon he would teach her, and she would know that he would've welcomed those binding ties. She would understand he'd left her in anger and wounded pride, and as blind as she.

"And what I did to you later, can you forgive that?" He could barely manage the words, but he had to ask. His life depended on her answer.

"There's nothing to forgive, darling. I had made a dreadful mistake. Nothing could change that, but I could try to ease the hurt. When you needed the words, for your pride, for your revenge, whatever the reason, I gave them. Gladly," she whispered. "I love you. I would give you my life if you asked it."

He looked into her shining face and knew her pride would lie in shreds in the dust at his feet if he asked it. But he wouldn't ask. It wasn't her pride he wanted; it was her love he wanted and needed. He knew it was his, only his, without reservation.

"Princess," he muttered, and a tear, hot and scalding, spilled down his cheek and over her fingers as he drew her into his embrace. His mouth was desperate against hers, hungry and shaken. If she loved him forever, it wouldn't be long enough.

Victoria was lost in the powerful circle of his arms, drawn tightly against him, his trembling body saying what he couldn't. She held him, soothing him, until the ravages of guilt were ended once and for all time by a love that survived. Long after his heaving body had quieted, she stood in his embrace, then at last she moved, slowly, subtly, withdrawing. He tensed, resisting, and she was gently insistent. With puzzled regret he lifted his head, then reluctantly let her slip free.

"I have on far too many clothes," she murmured as she stepped away, her fingers slipping beneath the opening of her shirt.

"No!" In a move as quick as it was astonishing, his hand stopped hers, closing over it with an unashamed tremor. "No," he said from the depths of a sweet new agony. "Let me."

She didn't hear the cry of the nighthawk, or see its shadow as it darkened the moon. She heard only the plea in Ben's voice and saw it echoed in his eyes.

Drawing her hand from his, she dropped her arms to her side. She was Victoria, woman, indomitable in yielding.

Ben hesitated. The fierceness of his passion leaped and soared in him like a torch burning in the wind. A look, half fearful, forewarned the driving power of a ravaging desire. It took her breath in an exultant cry.

Her cry released him from a prison of his own making. Hard, blunt, possessive fingers brushed aside her hair, caressed the uneven pulse at her neck, then slipped down her body. His palms rested and curved over the first swell of her breasts, delaying, savoring the instant when his blazing gaze would find no obtrusion. Together, as man and woman, fire and flame, they trembled on the brink for an eternity.

Then, with a breathtaking reverence, he brushed the fragile barrier from her shoulders and her arms, letting it fall forgotten at her feet. Victoria waited before him, clad only in moonlight.

They moved together urgently, clinging. Murmurs of loving and caring were cast amid tender, discovering caresses. Heart-shattering loneliness, fragments of misery and melancholy, tragic misunderstandings all blurred and faded, becoming just one small thread in the fabric of their lives.

"I'm not sure I can be gentle," Ben said against her lips. "It's been so long."

"I don't want gentleness." Victoria rose on tiptoe to match him kiss for kiss, passion for passion, with such intensity that he believed.

"I love you, Ben. I love you," she cried into the slanting pressure of his mouth.

Ben buried his lips in her hair. His grip on her shoulder would have been painful. His words were low and halting, a whisper in her ear. "Precious told me, and even Roarke. Once I thought I saw it in your eyes. Then…later you looked at me as if I was a devil…and I thought I'd killed anything you felt for me."

"You were my devil." She could tease about it now.

"And you were my princess." His hands began to move again in a sweet, roving caress.

He called her princess, and she heard and understood the endearment it had always been. *His princess.* That was all that mattered. Victoria smiled softly. Her hands burrowed beneath his shirt, her fingers stroking and exploring, becoming an instrument of madness. The exquisite pleasure was unbearable, the ache of a tormenting fever. Her hips arched into his, meeting the sensual demand of his lean body. Love and desire were a tangle never to be unraveled, and she would die of rapture.

"Ben." She called his name in the joyous freedom that honor had once forbade, even in delirium. "I don't want this to end."

"Hush." He brushed her lips with his. "Don't speak of ending. It's just begun." He led her over the polished pavers of the terrace floor to the open door of his room. Cool air flowed about them, touching Victoria's nakedness.

He sat her on his bed, leaning her against the thick pillows. With a seductive economy of motion his clothing disappeared from him. His body was a brand, the beat of his heart a primitive rhythm, when he came to her.

She welcomed him, knowing he neared the end of his endurance. Love was in her submission as she stroked his lips, curving her hand around his nape to draw him to her.

"Don't!" He groaned raggedly. "Don't touch me. Not yet. It's too soon. This must be slow and gentle, the loving we've missed all these years."

"We have all the time in the world for that, my darling. We'll have our gentle times. But please, not now."

His kiss was her triumph, eager and ravenous. She moved against him, searching, consuming, and in their desperate joining seemed to draw life from him. In their moment of ecstasy she captured his soul.

She called his name in the echo of a dream.

In the silvered light of predawn a breeze rose, twisting, swooping impishly, sending fallen leaves into a rustling swirl. A distant shutter banged to and fro. Trees swayed and dipped. As it had once before, a nightbird sang farewell.

Tangled sheets rippled as a mischievous gust found its way through the open door. Neither Victoria nor Ben felt its cooling rush as his hand trailed a familiar path, his longing to touch her insatiable.

Victoria's palm cupped the hard angle of his jaw, her fingers brushed against the roughness of its stubbled beard. She looked up at him steadily, her lips soft and curving. "There's been no one?" she asked in wonder.

"No one who mattered."

"Caroline?"

"There was little between us. I drifted along with her because—" He broke off and leaned to kiss her, his lips moving fleetingly over hers, saying what he left unsaid.

"And afterward?"

"There wasn't time. I had my work, then Lainie. It was enough."

Was it? The question hovered on her tongue but wouldn't come. Victoria turned out of his arms and moved away. She was absently graceful as she swung her feet to the floor and walked soundlessly, uncaringly naked, to the door.

The doubts she thought she'd put behind her ran rampant as the specter of the castle loomed before her. When the firestorm of their passion ebbed as she knew it must, what would remain? Would Ben again be obsessed? He coveted a castle; it lacked a princess. Would that obsession consume him? Would he become like her father, blinded by power and possession, forgetting love?

Behind her she heard the soft sounds Ben made as he approached her. She waited. A chain as delicate as a thread, as cool as a mountain stream, circled her throat before he slid his arm about her, drawing her back against his burning body. His cheek rested on her hair, his breath teasing the gleaming strands. "Once you left me, and until Lainie came, this was all I had of you. I meant to give it to her when she was older, but it would mean more if it came from her mother."

Victoria touched the heart that lay between her breasts and knew it held captive a unicorn, a magical creature. But was there enough magic in it for her? She shivered and clutched the arms that held her.

"Doubts after all, princess?" he asked gently.

She buried her cheek in the hollow of his neck. "I'm not really the princess; she never existed. If she had, the jungle would've destroyed her."

"I know that," he said. "Roarke told me."

"Roarke spoke. You listened, but did you understand? Can we be sure the day won't come when you'll discover I'm not the woman you thought? Will I become the stranger in your bed? We both know that would destroy us, and Lainie, as well. Would it be better for both of you if I left now?''

"And only destroy yourself.'' Ben spoke an irrefutable truth, then smiled to himself at her start of surprise. "You see, my princess, my dearest Victoria, I do know you.''

"Look.'' Victoria held up her hands. The scars were like shadows in the muted light. "These are a symbol of what I've become. I've seen a side of life that's harsh and unforgiving. I changed; I had to. Can you bear this ugliness?''

"Ugly? No, beautiful.'' His lips touched her cheek in a whisper of a kiss. His callused hand covered the taut flesh of her belly, tracing the smooth, silver striations left by his child. "Almost as beautiful as these.''

He ignored her gasp and moved his hands to her shoulders, turning her toward him. With a finger beneath her chin he lifted her face to his. "You were hardly more than sixteen when I first began to realize how much you meant to me. It was impossible; I knew that better than anyone. In the beginning I suppose I called you princess as a reminder of all the reasons I could never have you. Then a beautiful young girl took matters into her own hands, and princess became the name for the woman who would rule my heart.

"I love you, princess. I always have.'' His thumb brushed across her lips, which were bruised and pouting from his kisses. He looked long and searchingly at her and asked softly, "Can you leave me now?''

She felt the tears begin. They gathered on her lashes and spilled down her cheeks. Ben had said life held no guarantees. It was true. Each day brought its risks, and she would not lose her greatest treasure out of fear. "No," she whispered. "In a hovel or a castle, I could never leave you."

"No castles, sweetheart." Ben brushed her damp cheek. "Not for us. Not for our daughter. She already has the greatest heritage any child could have. A mother, so young and so brave, who fought all she'd ever known for the life of her child. With a love like that, what more could she need? What more could either of us need than to be loved as fiercely as my princess has loved us?"

"Do you mean that, Ben?"

"I've been a long time learning." His expression was grim for a fleeting moment, then it lightened with a smile. "But yes, I do mean it. I've finally seen how empty a life can be when possessions take the place of caring. Thank God, I had the best of teachers. I don't think our daughter will be quite as difficult to teach as the father."

A radiance filled Victoria's face. Her joy added an almost mystical richness to her happiness. Ben had seen that happiness before. It was in every look meant for Lainie. It was there when she gave herself to him. It was the happiness of loving and of giving.

"Our daughter," she murmured, and the happiness seemed to grow and explode inside her. "*Our* daughter. What a lovely sound."

"She's a lovely child, and will be even lovelier under your influence."

"Perhaps the first thing I should teach her is to chatter." Victoria made no effort to hide a glowing smile that was as impish as Lainie's could sometimes be.

"I knew it!" Ben groaned. "I knew that would come back to haunt me."

"No." Victoria sobered instantly. "No haunting, no ghosts. Not between us."

"No ghosts," Ben promised. "We're going to be far too busy loving each other to be bothered with them."

"Can we be sure, Ben. So much has happened."

"Shh, shh. The past doesn't matter anymore. Only one thing is really important now. Come here. Let me show you what I mean."

Like a lost child who's finally come home, she went into his arms, clinging to him as if she never meant to let him go. For a time Ben held her, rocking her, soothing her, murmuring promises she would never forget. As he kissed away a lingering tear, she knew the healing of love.

When Victoria slept, at last, in his arms, Ben watched, contentedly and eagerly, the dawning of the first day of their lives together.

Epilogue

A dios. I'll see you *mañana por la mañana.*" Lainie called.

Ben chuckled as he watched her racing past hedges and over flower beds. "Our daughter will soon be as fluent in Spanish as her mother."

"Roarke's children have been good for her," Victoria said fondly, using the name they'd given the people who'd come out of the jungle to study at the small school that was newly established in the castle. She looked up from the tiny garment she stitched and smiled across the terrace at Ben. "They've been good for all of us."

"You love offering them an opportunity to have better lives, don't you?"

"You know I do," Victoria admitted. "Thank you. For giving the castle to Roarke, for making it possible."

"I don't need castles; I have you," he teased, but Victoria heard the throb of truth in his banter.

"You certainly do. Have me, I mean." She blushed when he grinned at her choice of words, and rushed on. "What would we've done without Precious? Who but she could've organized the home skills class?"

"Or browbeaten the local farmers into demonstrating their farming methods?" Ben added, his wicked grin firmly in place.

"They love it. Every bit. The browbeating and the work."

"Of course they do, princess. Don't we all love the lives Precious has managed for us? Especially Lainie."

They waited as Lainie plucked a heavy-headed rose from its thorny stalk, then clattered up the stairs. A kiss aimed at her father's cheek landed in the vicinity of his chin an instant before she collapsed at Victoria's feet.

"For the prettiest mother in the world." She offered the pale pink rose with the special smile that was Victoria's alone. "And for Benji."

"Benji? Why that name?" Victoria asked.

"I think it'd be nice to name him after Daddy."

"Lainie, the baby could be a girl, you know," Ben said as he lounged against the stone balustrade, enchanted by the women in his life, wondering if a third could be as lovely.

His eyes met Victoria's over the black hair of their daughter. A tender look passed between them, one that trembled there each time Lainie's name was spoken. Lainie, the name Victoria had chosen. The name Ben had retained because she had chosen it. A small part of Victoria that he could give their child.

Lainie Stockton. Only a name to some, but to Ben and to Victoria, a gift of love.

"The next baby can be a girl, and we can call her Tory, but this one's Benji," Lainie prattled on, unaware of the moment shared by her parents. She patted the mound of Victoria's distended abdomen and gave them a smug look. The smile she flashed, now that she was eight going on nine, was not quite so gap toothed and grew, day by day, as lovely as Victoria's.

"Brat." Ben laughed again as Lainie rose and darted toward the kitchen, following a beckoning aroma.

In the hush that settled over them, he watched as Victoria worked, her needle flying in and out with incredible speed. Her hair, longer now, brushed against her cheeks. She'd laughed disparagingly over her girth, but Ben found her even more beautiful with his child.

So beautiful he ached for her.

With a quiet step he crossed the terrace and knelt before her, stilling the needle with a touch and a caress. "We have an hour before Jim arrives for dinner."

"What did you have in mind?" The sparkle of contented happiness matched the gleam in her eyes.

"I had in mind a bubble bath." Ben lifted a brow in a provocative tilt.

"With jasmine bubbles?"

"Is there any other kind?"

"Not for me," she said as her lips touched his in a fleeting kiss, remembering that first chaste bath and those in the years since, not so chaste. "Such a wicked man, tempting a woman in my condition."

"Your condition is wonderful," he admonished gently. "And I'm not half so wicked as I mean to be."

"Is that a promise?"

"A solemn promise, my love."

"Ahh." She turned her lips into the palm that stroked her cheek. "Then help me out of this chair, my wicked man, so that we might keep that promise."

"The pleasure's mine."

"Ours," she corrected him. "The pleasure's ours."

"Yes," Ben agreed as, with his arms about her, he led her from the terrace. "Ours."

 **Silhouette Desire**

COMING
NEXT MONTH

THERE ONCE WAS A LOVER—Dixie Browning
There once was a woman named Jo, who found she could never say no. Her love for Clay Abbott was more than a habit, she discovered he'd never let go!

FORBIDDEN FANTASIES—Gina Caimi
Was Ava's marriage a legend come to life? While filming a medieval love story of passion and betrayal, Ava found her own husband was the star of her wildest fantasies.

THEN CAME LOVE—Nancy Gramm
Maggie was determined to have a child, and Sam was exactly what she wanted in father material—for only one night. But with Sam, one night would never be enough.

JUST JOE—Marley Morgan
Quarterback Joe Ryan was the stuff women's dreams were made of...and he knew he could soothe Mattie's nightmares. But could he be her sweetest dream come true?

STOLEN DAY—Lass Small
A magical country fair brought Priscilla and Quinlan together. Quinlan insisted that she was the keeper of his quest and that his love would last a lifetime past their stolen day.

THE CHALLONER BRIDE—Stephanie James
Angie was destined to have a part in creating Flynn Challoner's empire, but she refused to marry for less than love...so why did she find herself dreaming of becoming a Challoner bride?

AVAILABLE NOW:

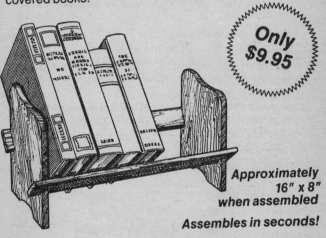

 *Silhouette Intimate Moments*

MARCH MADNESS!

Get Intimate with Four Very Special Authors

Silhouette Intimate Moments has chosen March as the month to launch the careers of three new authors—Marilyn Pappano, Paula Detmer Riggs and Sibylle Garrett—and to welcome top-selling historical romance author Nancy Morse to the world of contemporary romance.

For years Silhouette Intimate Moments has brought you the biggest names in romance. Join us now and let four exciting new talents take you from the desert of New Mexico to the backlots of Hollywood, from an Indian reservation in South Dakota to the Khyber Pass of Afghanistan.

Coming in March from Silhouette Intimate Moments:

SACRED PLACES: Nancy Morse
WITHIN REACH: Marilyn Pappano
BEAUTIFUL DREAMER: Paula Detmer Riggs
SEPTEMBER RAINBOW: Sibylle Garrett

Silhouette Intimate Moments, this month and every month.
Available wherever paperback books are sold.

IM-MM